D1736151

THE
HUNTRESS

BY THERESA HISSONG

Disclaimer:

This book is a work of fiction. Any resemblance to any person, living or dead is purely coincidental. The names of people, places, and/or things are all created from the author's mind and are only used for entertainment.

Due to the content, this book is recommended for adults 18 years and older.

©2018 Theresa Hissong

All Rights Reserved

ISBN: 978-1987529197

Cover Design:

Michelle Sewell

RLS Images Graphics & Design

Editing by:

Heidi Ryan

Amour the Line Editing

Dedication:

To the warrior in every woman…

Fight
Survive
Win

Contents

Foreword
From the Author…

The Huntress is a book about a woman who was brutally raped and left for dead at a young age. I wrote this book that way for a reason. It is a hard fact of life, and one that is easily ignored because people feel uncomfortable about the topic being brought up in conversation.

Sexual violence affects hundreds of men and women a day. If you or someone you know is a victim, please get help. There are organizations out there willing to help, and they have counselors on hand.

I've been wanting to write this story for a while. I decided that the Bad Girls collaboration was the perfect spot to tell Morgan Rayne's story. The main goal for me when writing this book was to show

how Morgan stood up and fought back for those who couldn't.

We started the Bad Girls brand to show that women are just as badass as men. I encourage you to check out the other books. Go to www.facebook.com/badgirlsbooks for more on the novels.

Thank you
Theresa Hissong

Disclaimer: This is a dark romantic suspense and there is mention of rape in this book. The content does not go into descriptions, and that is a choice I've made to be sensitive to victims should they read this story.

Prologue
Morgan
Seven Years Ago…

Dance practice is the only time I can be myself. When I work routines with my teammates, I forget about all the crap that is waiting for me when I leave the sanctity of my school. What kid actually enjoys school? I swear, I'm probably the only one.

I hesitate as I change clothes, knowing I can't get on the motorcycle in my shorts. It's too cold outside for me to ride without being covered. Two of my friends wave as they leave the locker room, and I momentarily yearn for their lives. They're in loving homes with both parents, and they don't fear for their lives every hour of the day. Reluctantly, I make slow work of tying my shoes because I don't want to leave. I know he's waiting out there for me.

"Come on, child," my coach whines. "I'd like to go home today."

"Yes, ma'am," I reply, and pick up my backpack. I guess I can't put it off any longer. It's time to leave.

The man waiting for me smells of cigarettes and beer. He runs the motorcycle club with my father and always picks me up from school. I have no one else. My mother is dead. I know my father killed her or had her killed. She was nothing to him, and now I am following in her footsteps. He will probably kill me, too.

The sound of his motorcycle sends bile into my mouth. He scares me, but I must obey. My father will make things worse for me if I don't. I rub absently at my collar bone where it was broken when I was ten. Yeah, my life sucks.

"Come on, little girl," Duke grunts as he drops his cigarette to the ground. "We have plans for tonight."

"Where are we going?" I ask, coming to stand next to him. The anchor tattoo on his neck pulses from the vein underneath. I've often fantasized about driving a knife into that very point, so I can watch him bleed out on the ground.

"Get on the fucking bike and don't ask

questions," he barks, grabbing my arm. I cry out from the pressure of his hold. I don't really have a choice when he yanks me toward his back. I climb on and hold on tightly as he speeds away from the school.

When we approach the clubhouse, I notice my father's bike is there, along with two others I don't recognize. When we enter the building, he's sitting at a table with two men from other MCs. Why are they here?

"The princess is home," Duke snickers. "Is it done?"

"What's done?" I ask, and immediately regret it when he backhands me. The impact is so hard, I fall to my knees and wipe my lip with the back of my hand. It's bleeding. I begin to stand, but Duke kicks me in the ribs.

"She's all yours," I hear my father say. He swats his hand out behind him, not even turning around to look me in the eye. "Do whatever you want with her."

"Father? Please don't," I gasp when Duke yanks me off the ground. A pinch registers in the back of my arm, and I look up at Duke to see him capping a syringe. "No..."

I feel him lift me over his shoulder and my body begins to relax. My back hits a mattress and I cannot move, but I know what he's doing. I cry, but no sound escapes me. I fight, but no movements come from my young body. I pray...but no one comes to save me.

Oh God....help...me...

Rain on my face wakes me from what I hope is nothing more than a horrible dream...a nightmare. Every bone in my body aches, and my jaw is unable to move to release the sound of my fear. I flex my hands, and the burning pain from my broken and torn nails causes me to suck in air through my cracked lips.

My mind tries to replay what happened to get me in this place...wherever it is. Pushing myself upright, my body sags to one side when the arm I'm using slips in the mud beneath me. *Where am I?*

I can't hear any sounds except for the hum of the rain. There are no lights, nothing but a black void. My knees are scuffed up, and most of my clothes are torn away from my body. A pain like no other flairs between my legs, and that's when I remember. Like a bad movie reel, my memories flash back

A man.

My father's right-hand man.

A needle.

His naked body over my virgin one.

Sleep.

Tears mix with the rain as I feel around for something solid to hold on to. If I can just find a phone, I can call for help. There's nothing around me but mud and maybe a few limbs. *Why is it so dark?*

I feel warmth rolling down my arms, my belly, and my face. Why is the cold rain not taking away the warmth? I don't understand.

The sound of an engine reaches my ears from what I can only guess is my grave. I search the darkness when the light from the passing vehicle above me shines brightly for a few seconds, quickly realizing I am down an embankment of some sort. I try to stand, but the pain in my stomach forces me back to my knees. I wipe the rain and mud out of my eyes, praying I can find my way out of this ditch.

He must've dumped my body once he was done. Maybe he thinks I'm dead? The various pains in my body are nothing compared to the knowledge that I was tossed out like yesterday's trash after he violated me.

It isn't until I try to climb the embankment that I realize the warmth is from blood…lots of blood. The pain in my belly is almost too much to bear as I being dragging my broken body out of my improvised grave. The scent of the earth rises up and tickles my nose when my fingers dig into the mud for traction.

I try to scream out when lights come around the corner again, but my jaw is frozen in place. It aches, and I just want to cry. I think it's broken. My wrist is surely fractured, my face is swollen, and I don't have the courage to see what damage there is to my abdomen.

I wish my momma was still alive, because I need her right now.

I don't know how long it takes me to crawl toward the road, but I breathe a sigh of relief when I sit down and lean my back against a sign indicating a curve is just up ahead. I make sure I'm facing the direction cars will be coming from and pray someone will see me. I can't move any further and standing up isn't an option. I know I must save myself, but at this point, I don't think I'm going to make it.

I cry harder when I remember how my father turned a blind eye earlier in the evening as I begged him to let me stay home and not go with Duke. His motorcycle friends are ruthless, and they'd touched me inappropriately too many times over the years. I should've known better when I heard him tell Duke, "She's all yours now." My father never cared for me, and then he gave me to this man to do with me as he pleased.

A scream wrenches from my throat the moment I see car headlights coming around the corner. I pray and keep chanting over and over in my head…*Please see me…Please see me.*

My hand raises in the air slightly before a new pain flares in my shoulder. I don't know if it's broken as well, but I need to make these people see me. I can't stay out here any longer. My body is starting to shiver and I'm bleeding everywhere.

Stars dance across my vision as the car's lights illuminate my body. Tears begin to fall harder when I hear the engine power down. Doors open and voices register, but the ringing in my ears makes it hard to understand what they're saying. Sirens wail off in the distance. The people are still talking to me, but I scurry out of reach when their hands seek to give me comfort. I don't want to be touched.

There is so much blood in my eyes, everything is blurry. More doors slam, and I blink to try and clear my vision. When I do, there is a female police officer in my face. Her mouth is moving, but I can't hear what she says.

All I can think about is how my father allowed this. He let Duke violate and almost kill me. Maybe they think I'm dead? Maybe I can get away from them now?

Oh my God! Maybe I can run away?

"Sweetheart," I hear the female officer say. It sounds like she's in a tunnel, but I can finally see her blurry face when she leans in closer. "Help is coming."

"Please," I mumble, being the only word my aching head and broken jaw can produce. "Please…please don't let me die."

Chapter 1
Morgan

My eyes scan the dark road, waiting for my chance to pounce. There are no sounds from passing cars; not even a whisper of the wind. No sounds of the night to hide me, but I do not need them to do what I came here to accomplish. He doesn't know I am in the shadows, patiently waiting to take him down. His world is about to be thoroughly changed when a female gives him a taste of his own medicine.

His name is Joshua McMillian, and he is wanted for domestic violence. He will be arrested and charged after I spend a little one on one time with him. Once the police pick him up, he will be in no better shape than his wife. She's currently in the ICU with a breathing tube down her throat because this fucking waste of space thought it'd be a good idea to strangle her after she served his dinner late.

My name is Morgan Rayne, and I have a reputation for being the one nobody messes with in this city. No one knows exactly who I am, what I do, or where I came from. And I want to keep it that way.

Joshua looks over his shoulder nervously as he fumbles with the key to his Mercedes. The light that shines on his car is bright against the darkness of the night. His face looks tired, and I can actually see the sweat beading up on his forehead from my position across the street.

Now is the time for me to make my move or he will flee. I've seen it too many times before. Men like him know they've done wrong and fear getting locked up. So, they run and hide. Usually the ones with loads of money fly away to a place they cannot be found. I have a feeling Joshua is one of them.

"What a pussy," I snarl under my breath.

I see my opening when he drops the keys, cursing when they slide underneath his car. My heart races and my fists clench at my sides. The adrenaline pulses through my system as I take off at a dead run. I take aim with a rock I had picked up from the neighbor's yard and throw it with accuracy, hitting and shattering the light as I come within feet of him.

He has no time to react as my fist contacts his

jaw. The asshole stumbles back as if he can't believe he is the one being hit. He doesn't speak, and that's okay, because I have plenty to say.

"How does it feel to be on the other end of a fist, Joshua?" I goad, taking another swing. This time, I land a direct hit to his left eye. The sting from the contact barely registers as I bounce back and forth from foot to foot.

"Who are you?" he demands, spitting blood on the concrete at my feet.

"I'm the one who is going to teach you a lesson," I reply, swinging my fist again, connecting with his stunned expression.

I expect him to at least swing back…maybe protect himself, but he doesn't. He continues to look everywhere but at me, the woman who is giving him a beat down. Ole Joshua is boring me.

"Your wife is fighting for her life because of you." I swing again, hoping to get some reaction out of him. My blood is pumping, and I need him to engage me in some sort of fight. This one-sided shit annoys me. "I'm here to give back what you gave her."

With that, I round on him, delivering a well-placed kick to his jaw, sending him to the ground. I only have a second to land on top of him and wrap my hands around his throat. As soon as the pressure registers, he begins to squirm.

"Please stop," he gurgles.

"Is this what Stacey said to you, asshole?" I growl, increasing the pressure. I know exactly how much strength to use to cut off the oxygen to his brain but not kill him. He will eventually pass out, and then I will be on my way.

"You bitch!" Ahhh, there it is. The real Joshua I was hoping for when I had come in search of him.

Joshua struggles beneath me. He's an average sized male, six feet two and probably two hundred pounds. He may outweigh me by sixty pounds, but I've been training and lifting weights since I was brutally attacked at the age of seventeen. This man is no match for me.

"Shit!" Sirens wail off in the distance, signaling that someone must have seen me and called the police. My little plan is going to be cut short.

I nail him one more time, relishing in the sound of a bone breaking in his jaw. The jackass starts crying, making me laugh one last time. "Have fun in jail, Joshua. I hope they treat you real good."

I push off him and stand, rearing back and kicking him between the legs so he doesn't try to move. He squeals loudly and rolls to the side. Blue lights bounce off the homes down the street, and that is my queue to go.

My feet are light, almost soundless, as I run around the side of his home, jumping the neighbor's fence. I've already planned my route of escape. In fact, I planned several. I know this city like the back of my hand and can find my way out of any situation. I've been doing it for years.

My car sits in a driveway of a home that had a for rent sign stuck in the yard when I arrived hours ago. I'd tossed it to the side, ensuring that no one would get suspicious of a vehicle sitting in the driveway of an empty home. I always make sure that my every move is calculated. In my line of work, one slip up could be deadly.

I slide behind the wheel of my car and crank it, wasting no time in backing out as calmly as possible despite my rapid heartbeat. As I turn on Maple Street, a police car passes me with his lights flashing. I wait until they are gone before I carefully return to my home. There is blood on my hands, and the last thing I need to do is drive recklessly and get pulled over by the cops.

My job for the night is done. I've delivered the message from Joshua's soon-to-be ex-wife's father who had hired me, and now it's time to move on to the next asshole on the never-ending list.

Unfortunately, there are several. It never ends.

* * *

Sun heats my skin as my eyes blink to clear the few hours I have slept. My blinds are drawn, but I don't remember doing it the day before. I keep my eyes closed and listen for any sounds. When I find none, I roll to my side, cursing when the broken spring in the couch imbeds in my side. I always live in fear that I will wake up and one of my targets will be sitting there waiting for me. If it wasn't for my body's natural instinct to sleep, I would go without. Being deep asleep is one of the biggest mistakes I can make.

My apartment is small, but that's all I need. I'm never home anyway, preferring to live in as much solitude as I can. It only takes me a few steps until I'm in my tiny kitchen, scooping up coffee grounds to pour into the coffeemaker. I haphazardly fill the machine with water, spilling some on the counter. As soon as I press the button, I stumble toward my bathroom while my morning breakfast brews as slowly as humanly possible.

Grabbing up my phone, I return to the kitchen and lean against the counter, looking to see if I missed any messages during my three hour nap. It doesn't take long before I find the news article talking about Joshua's arrest when I scan the local newspaper's website. His mug shot makes me cringe.

Under the cover of darkness, you don't notice much of a person's face. Now that it's in bright colors, I actually feel a little bad for the beat down I gave him the night before. The article goes on to say that the suspect seemed to have been in scuffle right before he was arrested at his residence. There is no mention of me or my little visit.

Good boy, Joshua.

I flip over to my bank's online access and see that Stacey's father has wired the money for my services. I refuse to even look at the current balance, but it does register that there are six figures sitting there collecting dust. I don't do this for the money, but the families who find me through…well, let's say less than appropriate channels, seem to use my payment as some sort of closure. I use only the minimum amount of funds to live on, and the rest I will donate anonymously to a charity of my choosing later in the year.

I flex my right hand as I hold my coffee in my left. There are bruises forming on my knuckles, but that's just part of the perks of what I do. I'd hoped to make it to the gym today to spar with my trainer, but he would just turn me around and tell me to go home when he sees the damage.

With a heavy sigh, I shuffle my feet forward and make my way toward the freezer. I dump the ice tray into a plastic bag and tie it closed. Cursing, I place the pack over my knuckles and twist a clean dishrag around it, holding the bag in place. I hope it will work over the next few hours, so I can go into the Quarter without any signs that I have been in a recent fight.

My phone rings as it's sitting on the couch next to me. I set my coffee aside and pick it up. The caller is listed as unknown, but I already know it will be another possible client. I do not have friends, and even if I did, I'd know their numbers by heart. Another bad decision would be to have people who know me programmed into my personal phone. That's like a road map to my whereabouts…and I don't want to be found.

"Yeah," I mumble into the phone.

"Um," the shaky female voice on the other end says. "I'm looking for an exterminator." The underground calls me all sorts of things: exterminator, cleaner, huntress.

"I can help you," I reply, leaving the line open

for the person on the other end to give me all the details.

"My daughter was attacked and left for dead," the female continues. She sniffles a few times as she composes herself enough to continue. "The man responsible has gone missing, and I hear you can help me find him."

"Tell me what's going on," I urge.

"Brooke has been seeing this guy," she begins, the nervousness in her voice changing from scared to angry within seconds. One thing I've learned over the years is that a mother will do anything to protect her child. Too bad my own mother wasn't around to protect me. "He's a piece of shit. She left with him last week, and we hadn't heard anything until the police showed up at our door at midnight. She's at the trauma center. He…he violated her and tossed her body in a ditch outside the city. I want him taken out."

"I'm so sorry," I answer. The stories of these women are almost always the same. The same as mine, but I must push my memories away and focus on what needs to be done. "Give me his name."

"They call him Vyper," she answers. "I don't even know his real name, but he is part of the security team at Club Phoenix on Bourbon Street."

"I know where that is." I cringe. Vyper is a part of the biggest club in the French Quarter. I can find him and take him out, but I'll have a hard time getting through the goons who watch over the place where he works. Club Phoenix is notorious for the copious amounts of drugs that filter through the joint on any given night. The man who owns the club is just as elusive as I am, and I've never seen him in person, but I know he's there every single night, watching over his gang of muscled security. Those men are brothers through the blood they beat out of their clients who don't pay up when the drugs are sold.

"I'll pay you a million dollars," the mother says through gritted teeth. "I don't care what you do as long as he is no longer a problem."

"I'll send you the information." I hang up and look in the bathroom mirror. My tired face stares back at me, knowing I must prepare to go on the hunt again. I don't even bother asking her for money up front. I would do it for free if it would give the victim a sense of peace knowing the man who violated her wasn't breathing anymore.

This time, I gather my keys with dread and walk out the door, knowing that one of these days, I will die doing what I can to avenge those who are speechless.

I shake off the visions that creep into my head, reminding me of the hell that made me who I am today. It doesn't matter, because I have dedicated my life to saving the women in this city…the ones who have been victimized. Just like a vampire, I hunt in the dark, stalking the monsters and calculating the perfect time to strike.

This is who I am. This is what I do.

I am *The Huntress*.

Chapter 2
Morgan

In New Orleans, summer lasts until after Thanksgiving, but on this September night, the heat is bearable. I've pulled my hair back into a ponytail with the hair tie I religiously keep around my wrist and tuck it up into an old trucker hat, pulling it down low over my eyes. The sun is setting as I turn onto the infamous Bourbon Street in the heart of the French Quarter. Tourists step out of my way as I walk toward the bar like they know I'm not one to toy with even at this early hour. Locals give me a wary nod and go on about their business. Again, they know I am trouble, and they keep their distance.

I do not slow as I approach Club Phoenix, but I do watch out of the corner of my eye as I pass. Jackson Pace, the owner, has recently spent some money to fix the place up. If I were a different person and had actual friends to go out with, this would be the place to go. It is the hottest bar in the Quarter, and if you're willing to pay the exorbitant prices for the booze or even splurge for a VIP section, Club Phoenix would be your kind of entertainment.

There is a man standing at the entrance. He's tall and muscular, his skin is a beautiful, rich mocha color and his eyes are golden brown. The doorman gives my body an appreciative glance and continues watching the few people who are shuffling down the street. The music inside is at a normal level at this time of the afternoon, and I notice a few people sitting at the bar, but nothing inside piques my interest. I do not know what Vyper looks like, and for all I know, the guy at the door could be him.

As soon as I make it to the next road, I turn left and find my way to a jewelry shop up the road. The bell over the door announces my arrival, and I walk up to the counter. The old man standing behind it is the only person in this town who knows me very well.

"Well, hello *cher*," Landry says, then winks. "What brings you by the shop today?"

Landry Pierre sees all and knows all in the Quarter. His life outside of this place is unknown to anyone. The man's reputation is about the same as my own, but he's been here a hell of a lot longer than I have. No one messes with Landry, and from what I've witnessed over the years, I can attest to his notoriety.

"I'm looking for someone," I say after I look around the shop to make sure we are alone.

"Ah," he grunts, and his bushy eyebrows push forward. "You are looking for trouble."

"I'm looking to right a wrong, Landry," I grit out through my clenched teeth. I have not seen this girl, or the damage done to her. I don't need to see it, either. Every time I close my eyes, I remember my own injuries like it was yesterday.

"You know? One of these days, your acts of vengeance will be your demise. You know this, right, Morgan?" he questions, his left brow rising high into his hairline. Landry is old enough to be my grandfather, and his philosophical messages are rampant whenever I am around.

"That will be all on me then, Landry," I reply, blowing out a breath. "I need to know if you can tell me anything about a man named Vyper who works at Club Phoenix."

"No, no," Landry gasps, waving his hands out in front of himself like he's trying to ward off a bad spirit. "You need to stay outta dat club, little one. Dat is Jackson's man, and you let him deal with Vyper." Landry's Cajun accent thickens as he narrows his eyes at me. I am not going to be swayed by his attempt to father me.

"Yes," I growl, clenching my fists as they sit on top of the counter. "You either tell me about him, or I will walk into that club tonight and start asking my way."

"Girl, you are so *tete dure*," he sighs. He uses the Cajun term for being stubborn, and I have to laugh because he is right.

"Are you going to tell me or not?" I push, knowing he will tell me what I want to know even if he doesn't like it.

"Vyper is a nickname for a reason," he begins, pulling a stool over to sit on behind the counter. I lean my elbow on the top of his old cash register and listen. "He's a mean son of a bitch, Morgan. He's bald, with tattoos all over his head where his hair should be. He's missing his right pinky finger, and if that doesn't give him away, the fact that his teeth have been filed down to sharp fangs will confirm it for you."

"How did he lose his pinky?" I ask, genuinely curious. I've seen a lot of strange people since coming to this town three years ago. The teeth and tattoos don't surprise me.

"The owner of Club Phoenix, Jackson Pace, did it," Landry responds, shaking his head in disappointment. "That boss of his is so dangerous, it makes Vyper look like a marshmallow."

"Damn," I sigh. "Do you know where Vyper stays?"

"Yes, but he hasn't been around for two or three days, though." Landry shrugs. "Heard Jackson is looking for him, too."

"Well," I drawl, frustrated with Landry's lack of information. "Where does he actually live? I need to go by his place to see if I can find him."

"He has an apartment in town, but lives above Club Phoenix," he says, then nods toward the direction of the club. I curse under my breath because it doesn't look good that I'll be able to catch him away from the club. "Does this have anything to do with the young woman he was seeing? Heard she tried to leave him. Now, no one has seen her around, either."

"She's recovering from being brutalized by this asshole," I snarl. "His time is coming to an end real soon, Landry."

"No man should do that to a female," he says

sadly. Landry stares off over my shoulder for a few seconds before shaking his head and looking into my eyes. "You be damn careful, and you know where to find me."

"Thanks," I say, straightening up and leaning over the counter to kiss the old man's weathered cheek. He smells of incense and knowledge, and I find that comforting. He is the only man in my life I trust, but even with Landry, I am leery of the things he tells me. I wouldn't put it past him to lie to me to keep me out of trouble. Like now, I must go find this guy, and I pray that the information he provided is going to help me.

I know this will be hard to accomplish, but I am determined to give that poor girl and her family closure. No matter what happens in a court of law, Vyper will most likely be slapped on the back of the wrist and let go after a short stint in prison. The mother made it perfectly clear that she wants her daughter's attacker gone, and I agree with her.

Sometimes, I am asked to give life lessons to these scumbags who abuse their wives or girlfriends. Other times, I am paid highly to go a step further.

This is not the first time I have killed a man for the things he has done.

And it won't be the last.

Chapter 3
Jackson

The bass from the music in the club below my office vibrates the floor as I pace in front of my desk. Club Phoenix is full of people tonight, and the cash is flowing in at a steady pace, but my mind is on cleaning up a mess within my circle. One of my men has jeopardized my operations here by hurting a female, leaving her for dead.

I take a seat behind my desk and rub my temples to relieve some of the tension. The music below usually doesn't bother me, but tonight I am wound up tighter than usual. The shot of whiskey at my side does nothing to calm the darkness inside of me.

I flip through the photos again, swallowing hard to keep the contents of my stomach from retching back up. The images before me are disturbing, and I've killed men before. I've seen the worst that can be done to a human body, but this…this is unnerving even for me.

"I want to know where he is now!" I slam my hand down on the desk for good measure and also to burn off the anger inside me. Rocco walked in minutes ago with photos of a woman lying beaten and bloody in a hospital bed. The suspect is one of my enforcers, and I want him dead.

"No one has heard from him, and his cell phone was traced to a trashcan three blocks from here," Rocco growls. "He left in a hurry, and I can guarantee he knew you'd punish him for the things he's done to this poor woman."

My employees are some of the deadliest men in New Orleans. They've done the things I've asked of them to keep my underground businesses running smoothly for years. This man, however, broke my one rule.

We do not hurt women… ever.

Cyrus, my right-hand man and the VP of my operations, is standing to my right as he takes a look at the photos. I don't even need to look at him to know he's just as pissed as I am, because I can feel the anger radiating off of him like heat from a stove set on high.

"Check all of the places he usually hangs out," I order, ticking off places where he might be hiding. "I want all of the cameras at my warehouses and the ones here at the bar checked thoroughly. He is not allowed anywhere near my properties."

"Yes, sir," both men reply at once.

"Roman is checking his apartment in the city and should be here soon," Cyrus informs me. Good thing Roman is on top of things, because the more people I have working to find this waste of space, the quicker I can put Vyper down.

"Jackson," Moose, one of my enforcers, interrupts. The music below is getting louder as the night progresses, but I'm too worked up over the disappearance of Vyper to be excited for the thick crowds below. "Lola called up to say that you have a suspicious person in the club."

Lola oversees the main bar, and she does the books for me every night. She's been a part of my team for the last six years, ever since I purchased this club to run a legitimate business. If someone walks into my club and doesn't belong, she will be the one to surely notice. That woman is my bloodhound, and I trust her wholeheartedly.

"Who?" I ask, wondering if it has anything to

do with Vyper.

"I checked the monitors, and I recognize the woman. She's called 'The Huntress'," Moose states, then frowns. "Want me to keep an eye on her?"

"The Huntress?" I ask, narrowing my eyes.

I've heard of her, and she's deadly. Apparently, she is a hired hitman…well, hitwoman, and she doesn't show mercy to the men she is after. The fact that she shows up in my club a few days after my guy has gone missing tells me that she has more than likely been hired by the family of this young woman.

"She's a goddamn hitwoman," I snarl, standing up from my desk. "I'm going out on the floor for a drink. I want to see her for myself."

All of my men nod and wait at the door for me to be ready to go. They'll need to work as my protection when we go downstairs to mingle with the patrons. It's for my safety. I've dealt in many illegal activities in this town and some disgruntled people would be delighted to see me out in the open and unprotected.

"What's the game plan?" Cyrus asks as I descend the stairs to the club floor. We exit through an unmarked door, and my men surround me as we head toward the VIP section. I don't look for the huntress right away. I don't want her to catch on to us knowing she is lurking in my club.

Roman is coming in the front door as we head toward my seat, falling in line to my left as he intercepts us. "Unable to locate him, boss."

"Find him," I bark.

I see her at the bar as I walk by. Lola is watching her but gives me a short nod as I pass to indicate the woman in question. She is wearing a flashy top and short shorts with thigh high boots. She's trying to look like she belongs in the crowd of club goers, but her aura screams danger. Even I can feel her power from this distance.

I hear a few women giggle as I continue toward the VIP section, and I ignore the stares. I'm an elusive man and one they will never catch. It's not that I don't like women, but the bimbos frequenting my business are nothing but gold-diggers and not worth my time.

As soon as I slide into the booth, Marcy hands me a scotch on the rocks. I nod my thanks and she walks away. I raise a brow when Cyrus and Roman come to stand next to me. The huntress is out of my line of sight, but I know my men are well aware of her position.

"I want a word with her," I say, tossing back

my drink.

"We know nothing about her," Cyrus warns.

"Wait until the time is right, and then take her up to my office," I order. "Be cautious, she has a reputation for being deadly."

"We will meet you in the office," Roman says, then nods and turns away.

The Huntress, better known as Morgan Rayne, has stepped on my turf, and now the ball is in my court. She either knows where Vyper is, or she's in my club thinking I am keeping him hidden. Regardless, I will be the one to capture my man. She needs to know she is treading on thin ice when it comes to him.

He is deadly.

I'm even deadlier.

Chapter 4
Morgan

It's the day after I talked to Landry, and I have spent most of the early morning hours watching Vyper's apartment in New Orleans. Sadly, there'd been no activity and I headed home an hour before the sun came up to grab some food and sleep.

Brooke's mother had obtained a throw away phone, and she sent photos of her daughter to me sometime around nine this morning, knowing that any communication between us could be brought to light if the law comes asking questions when Vyper is found. I have been staring at the wall in my apartment for the past two hours, trying to wash away the images I'd seen. My index finger and thumb pinch at the hair tie on my wrist, popping it repeatedly against my skin as I think. The burn of tequila doesn't help with that at all. I pour another double shot in an attempt to dull my feelings.

I never thought I would see another woman's injuries look close to what I'd endured, but I was proven wrong when I saw what Brooke looked like when she was finally brought to the hospital. There isn't a spot on her body that wasn't bruised, cut, or brutalized. If her mother hadn't told me that she had survived, I'd have thought I was staring at the pictures of a woman who'd been brought into the morgue.

It's after eleven when I finally put on my boots, dropping my Glock down into a holster built into the right side. The leather comes up and over my knees, ensuring no one would know what I have hidden inside. My black shorts are made of stretchy material, so I still have range of motion in the event there is a need to defend myself. My top is blood red and cut low into my cleavage. I pull my black and silver-streaked hair over one shoulder to make myself appear sexier and spend a good amount of time on my makeup. I need to look like I fit in at Club Phoenix when I arrive there to search for Vyper.

I live six blocks from Bourbon Street in an old apartment over a noisy restaurant. I lock my door as I exit, testing the knob twice to make sure the lock has engaged. Before I step away, I take my hand and run my fingers over the hair tie that stays permanently on my wrist. I use it when I go after a mark. It ensures that my hair is out of hand's reach and I don't get blood in my hair. I take the narrow steps down to the street below and push open the gate that keeps the public out of the residential part of the building. I tug on the metal bars twice, again reassuring it is secure as well.

A homeless man is sitting upright against the wall by the door, his head hanging down as he sleeps soundlessly. I drop a ten dollar bill into the cup he is holding tight against his chest. Even in sleep, he knows to keep his belongings close, because at any time, it could be taken away from him.

Several horse and buggy carts greet me as I venture further into the Quarter. I know some of the drivers, but we only nod in passing. The heels on my boots click with each step I take. A few frat boys stop to stare and whistle in my direction. When my eyes make contact with the biggest one in the group, he freezes and holds his hand out, blocking his buddies from moving in my direction. I see his head give a short jerk before the others stop their cat calls and move out of my way.

As I turn onto Bourbon Street, the waves of

people slow my descent into the darker recesses of the town I call home. Several women are standing in the middle of the street, stumbling around with their clothes in disarray from flashing their breasts at men who have gathered on the balconies of the bars, throwing beads for a few seconds of visual gratification.

I watch them from the corner of my eye, hoping the throngs of men who walk by don't reach out and touch them. These women are vulnerable, and I hope like hell their friends are there to keep them close. A drunk female who walks around on her own is nothing more than a moving target. The only thing that keeps me from approaching them is the fact that I spot their friends standing close by and hurrying out to grab them. I really hope they are going back to their hotels.

As I walk, I keep my head lowered, but my eyes still scan my surroundings. A dark-skinned Haitian man stands at the entrance of his gift shop, looking on at the people who shuffle down the street with drinks in hand. A strip club up ahead has four humongous men standing guard at the doors, checking identifications and taking money. One of them watches me as I pass, but quickly loses interest when a drunken man, who's old enough to be my father, stumbles up and pays his way in the door.

The music from Club Phoenix is loud and overpowers everything within a block of its doors. Strobe lights cast white light out onto the sidewalk, and from the street, you can see a stage with two people standing on a raised floor. A man and woman keep the party going by pulling a few patrons up to dance provocatively for half a song before sending them on the way.

I flash my driver's license at the man who works the door. It is fake, just like everything in my life. I cannot be known to anyone. He gives me a onceover and steps to the side, allowing me entry. The music vibrates through my chest, but I don't let it bother me. I've been in these clubs too many times to count. In all of the bars on this road, and as the night wears on, the music is turned up so the patrons are too pumped to leave, making them spend more money on booze.

The first order of business is to look for exits and see who is posted at each one. I am disappointed to see security is tight in this place, but that will not deter me. I need to find Vyper. Landry said that I wouldn't be able to miss him. Tattoos and a bald head. That can't be too hard, right?

The back bar is swarming with college-aged

men and women. A man in jeans and a shirt with the logo of the bar on it stands at the end next to a door clearly marked as a fire exit. There are two more bars in the club, all with the same type of security guy standing close. My eyes track two other men as they make their way toward the bathrooms in the back of the club. The men turn just before they reach the men's room and open an unmarked door. On the other side, a man greets them and puts his wrist to his lips, telling me they have some type of communication system in place.

Not good at all.

All of the men are rough looking with tattoos covering most of their exposed skin. Their hands and knuckles are also inked. Each one has a decent haircut, which makes me believe that at least Jackson Pace wants his employees to have some sort of businesslike qualities. But what about Vyper? Where does he fit into this?

I saunter up to the bar closest to the door the men entered, guessing that is the way to the private offices of the owner. There's no way I'll be able to get past them if they are holding Vyper inside and keeping him from being seen. If Jackson Pace is harboring this asshole, I might even give him an ass kicking just for being involved. Trouble is my middle name, but tonight I want to be invisible. A guy stumbles away, leaving me a space to slide in so I can lean my arm against the bar.

"What'll you have, doll?" the female bartender asks. She is tall and super slender. Her hair is in jet black braids down to her waist, like a gothic Farrah Fawcett. She's wearing minimal makeup, but she doesn't need any to enhance her beauty. The shirt she is wearing is similar to the security team's, but hers has been cut to reveal her shoulders and is tied in a small knot just under her bountiful breasts.

"Rum and Coke," I yell over the music. She quickly makes my drink and hands it over. I pay her and drop a healthy tip into the plastic jug in front of me.

"What brings you in here?" she questions.

"Looking for a good time," I say with a smile, wondering if she is going to offer me some of the drugs her boss runs through this place.

"Well, this is the place," she laughs.

I thank her again for the drink and turn around to watch the crowd. Bodies are pressed together as the club music blares. It isn't my usual style of music, but it's what pumps up the customers. If I didn't know anything about the reputation of the place, just like ninety percent of the people in here, I'd give the guy credit for what he has created.

A man stumbles into my side, taking a moment to rake my body with his glassy stare. I snarl in his direction, sending him back a few steps. He mumbles something before shuffling toward the men's restroom.

I see the unmarked door open out of the corner of my eye. My hope is that Vyper will show himself. I want to get up close and personal with him, using my looks and body to do what I can so he will find me interesting enough to strike up a conversation. Yes, I've used my looks to sway the men I'm after. I learned a long time ago that these types of monsters are ruled by their dicks and how much they want to sink them into a warm pussy.

When a man emerges, I am taken aback. He's not like the security guards. No, this man looks more like a rockstar, and I mentally run images through my mind, trying to place who he might be, but come up empty-handed. He's tall and tattooed everywhere. The backs of his hands are inked, but I can't make out exactly what the design is from my position. Two security guards close in on him and start pushing through the crowd. As they approach, I set my drink on the bar top and pretend I am invisible.

"Unable to locate him, boss," one of the

guards says as they pass.

"Find him," the rockstar guy responds. His voice is like velvet, and for a moment, I am enchanted by it. His scent drifts across my nose as he passes, and it is enticing, like a magical potion. More guards surround him, and they push patrons out of the way so the man can pass.

It doesn't take me long to realize that the guy is probably Jackson Pace. As I watch him head over to the VIP section, my suspicions are confirmed when he is waved through and stops and shake hands with everyone seated in the area. More security surround him as he slips into an empty booth. A waitress hurries over and sets a drink in front of him without waiting for payment.

"Oh, that's Jackson," a woman swoons next to me. "He's delicious."

"He's so off limits, I'd have to pay to get close to him," her friend complains. "I don't have that type of money, but if I did, I'd spend it all on him."

"Investments are really good sometimes," the swooning woman chuckles.

I roll my eyes and turn back to the bar. The bartender slides over another drink. I toss back the liquid and ignore the burn from the alcohol. She's made this one stronger, and when I look over at her, she smiles and wipes down the bar top.

Music pulses the closer I move toward the dance floor. More people have entered the club, and you cannot miss the rise in temperature as you approach the bodies that are pushed together. Different colored lights swirl around, hitting the walls, people, and the floor in no certain order. A popular dance song is playing over the speakers, but quickly changes into some type of remix. The club goers must love it because they begin to jump and cheer, some of them singing along with the song. If I was a different person and had time to spend on myself, I'd be on the dance floor with them.

I look over my shoulder and see that Jackson is listening to one of his goons, then I see his eyes scan the dance floor. I immediately duck behind two tall college boys in the hope that I'm not seen. This could be my only chance to get into the bowels of this place while the boss is away.

I walk over to one of the doors marked as an exit. I linger there for about two songs, sipping on what's left of my watered-down drink. Just as I turn to set the drink on a nearby table, a heavy hand lands on my shoulder. I stiffen, knowing that I should act the part of a stunned club goer. If I actually defended myself, everyone would see this asshole go down.

"The boss wants to see you," a gravelly voice states from behind me.

"I don't know your boss," I reply, pivoting my foot so I can turn around to face him. Before I make my move, the guy wrenches my arm behind my back and presses his body close. I count to three and lift my foot.

"Ah, ah, ah," he warns, just as the door behind him opens and he jerks me back, kicking the door closed with his foot. A cloth sack is pulled over my head, and I feel rope at my wrists. I try to kick out at my captor, but another man grabs my ankles, lifting me off the floor.

I keep quiet, using my senses to listen to my surroundings. The men are silent as they tie up my wrists, but not my ankles, and start moving. I know I should fight, but I'm in the inner sanctum of Club Phoenix and one step closer to my mark. They obviously know who I am, and I'm going to use that to my advantage.

They think they have me in their web, but I'm as lethal as they are.

It's time to find the man they call Vyper.

Chapter 5
Jackson

Morgan Rayne is feisty and the sight of her fighting the restraints gives my body and mind a thrill I haven't felt in a very long time. I know she is deadly, but she doesn't know that I know who she is, and I can use that to my advantage.

"Let me the fuck go!"

I carefully remove the cloth bag from over her head and take a stand in front of her as she continues to kneel at my feet. When her eyes blink to clear her vision, I am taken aback by the bright blue that looks up at me in anger. She is even more stunning than I'd ever imagined. Her reputation had made me think she was much larger, more muscular, than the woman before me.

She's on her knees, and the sight is just

another reason for my cock to harden at my wayward thoughts. The huntress before me is not like other women who've entered my club. I've heard of the things she does, and I am impressed by her abilities. She is a killer. Only those who are privy to the inner workings of this city know of her deeds, and she's really good at staying in the dark and off the authority's radar. Her secrecy intrigues me.

"What are you doing in my club?" I circle around her, careful not to touch her skin. She is tattooed on one arm and her dark hair is offset with a few silver streaks down the back. Her lips are full, and I stifle a groan when her pink tongue snakes out to wet them seductively. One second she looks like a man's fantasy, and the next, the corner of her lip lifts in a snarl.

"Having a fucking drink," she replies, and I see fire in her eyes. "Is this any way to treat a customer, asshole?"

I adjust myself once more before walking forward to cup her jaw. The tips of my fingers tingle with awareness from the connection. I tsk softly as I tighten my hold to ward off the feeling of her softness. She needs to understand that the only other person deadlier than her...is me.

"My name is Jackson Pace, and I want to

know who you are searching for in my club."

She purses her full lips together, and I see her jaw flex as she clamps down her teeth. She's not willing to talk, but I have ways of making people do what I need them to do. "I can make you talk."

"There's nothing you can do that hasn't been done to me in the past, *Jax*," she snarls. I twist my head from side to side at hearing that nickname. I hate it. I despise it, actually, but for some reason, I like the way it sounds coming from her smart mouth.

Her statement stops me from continuing for a moment. She's tough for a reason, and the reason is not one I'd wish on anyone. Her single statement tells me everything I need to know about her and what she does in the city. She's a vigilante.

Two of my men are standing guard at the door to the office. Rocco and Moose are fairly new to my team. They've seen me kill someone for being disrespectful to my face. They've seen me torture a man for rolling his eyes, too. Both men raise a brow at me when I don't immediately correct her for using the name.

I nod toward the door and dismiss them, leaving me alone with Morgan. I already know why she is here, but I need to hear it come from her own lips. Vyper is in enough trouble that there has been a hit taken out on him, and Morgan Rayne is acting as the Grim Reaper for my estranged enforcer.

"You going to untie me?" she asks, narrowing her eyes. I see her shoulders move slightly, and I know she is trying to release herself, but the binds are solid, I have no doubt in my men's abilities.

"Not until you tell me what you're doing in my club, Ms. Rayne," I reply.

"Well, I shouldn't have to answer your question," she replies. "If you know who I am, then you obviously know who I'm looking for. Let's not play games here, Mr. Pace."

"The man you are looking for is mine, and I will handle him once he returns," I offer, knowing she will bite when I lay down my knowledge of why she's here, and I'm right.

"Ah," she chuckles, "no. Vyper is mine."

"Do you know *anything* about this man?" I ask, taking a seat in a high-backed chair across from her. I prop my ankle over my other knee and sit up straight, enjoying the way she looks kneeling in the center of my office.

"Don't need to," she says as she shrugs one shoulder. "He is a waste of fucking space. I'm not here to know if he knits with his grandma or gets railed in the ass by his co-workers."

I chuckle at her words. She's harsh… and I like that.

"You are quite savage," I surmise.

"You have no idea, Jax," she smirks. "Why don't you untie me, and we can see who walks out of here first to find the man I came for?"

Chapter 6
Morgan

I'm in a room that looks more like an extravagant office than the musty dungeon my mind had conjured up while I was blindfolded. I quickly glance toward the door and realize we are alone. I don't know if there are any guards on the other side of the door, but I know I can get through them. For the moment, I will wait. I know when not to attack.

"Take a seat over there, Morgan," he says from his desk.

When I expertly climb to my feet even with my hands still tied behind my back, I watch as he scoots his chair up close to his expensive desk. He has changed his clothes since I saw him in the club. He's now in a sleeveless shirt, and his arms are covered in tattoos over his defined muscles. I close my eyes momentarily, trying to calm my erratic heartbeat. It doesn't work. His dark emerald eyes catch mine when I open them again and move toward the chair he indicated with his chin. It's hard not to stare at him, but I resist and take a seat.

"You cannot hold me hostage," I say with strength behind my voice.

"I never said you were," he says, them smiles. My lower belly flutters from the sight. Jackson Pace is extremely good looking. His jet-black hair curls ever so slightly at the base of his neck, and I notice his lip is pierced. *Fuck me.* He looks nothing like a wealthy club owner.

"Then why am I still bound?"

"For your safety," he replies, leaning over to rest his elbows on the desk. I wiggle my fingers to find some sort of give in my bindings. I'm able to get my thumb through a loop to feel where it is tied. "And mine."

"So, here we are." I smile, using my blue eyes to gain his attention. His gaze drops to my lips, and I feel the corner of my lip raise. I'm being only slightly seductive, but it has an effect on him. I see it in the way his eyes heat. "I assure you, Jax, I am not here to harm you."

"Hmm, so what do you know about my

enforcer?" he asks. The man wants what information I have on Vyper, but I don't have any. He doesn't need to know that, however.

"Nothing," I shrug, feeling the rope give just the slightest at my wrist.

"I'm assuming you've been paid to kill him," he states, not caring to form it as a question. I have underestimated Jackson Pace. It seems he knows me better than I realize.

"My business with Vyper is none of yours," I reply, feeling the binds at my wrists loosen fractionally.

"That's where you are wrong." He leans back in his seat, resting his elbows on the arm of the chair and steeples his fingers so he can press them to his lips. I see the hoop in his lip move, and I take stock of that tiny bit of information. He doesn't have a great poker face. The little tic of rolling the piercing with his tongue gives away his uncertainty. This man is as clueless as to Vyper's whereabouts as I am. "He is very dangerous, and I am his boss. He belongs to me, and he's broken the one rule that I demand of my employees."

"What's that?" I smirk. "Not showing up for a shift?"

"Hurting a woman," Jackson replies, his eyes

darkening with his confession. It shocks me. Jackson Pace, the leader of illegal activities in the Quarter, has morals?

"I did not expect that answer from you." I nod, indicating my binds. "Since you tied me up like a prisoner."

"I will let you go once you promise me that you will leave Vyper to me," he vows, standing from his throne.

"I have a job to do, and he is mine." I shrug, unwinding the rope around my wrists. I pause in my speech to bring my hands around in front of my body, dropping the rope to the floor. I waste no time in reaching for the small pistol I keep in my boot, raising it to point at his head. "I appreciate our little meeting, but I will be leaving now, Jax."

Jackson raises his hands and nods toward the door. "My men are on the other side of that door."

"Call them in and tell them to back the fuck off," I snarl, moving off to the side of the room and position my back to the wall, so I can keep the door and Jackson Pace in my field of vision. He smiles with pride, like he approves of my training.

"I'm going to press this button on my phone," he says, moving his hand slowly. On my nod, he presses the button. When a male's voice comes over the line, he gives the order. "Ms. Rayne will be leaving."

"Yes, sir," the voice replies. Two heartbeats later, the door opens to reveal a huge man with short black hair and a scar through his upper lip. He starts to reach for something in his coat, probably a gun, but Jackson stops him. "No, Cyrus."

Cyrus nods and steps aside, keeping his hands away from his coat. My eyes narrow as I begin to walk toward the door. I'm almost to the threshold when Jackson calls out, "I will be seeing you again soon, Ms. Rayne."

Chapter 7
Jackson

"You just let her walk out of here!" Cyrus barks. My bodyguard is pissed. I don't blame him, but I have to let her go. I wasn't lying when I said we didn't hurt women.

Morgan Rayne is lethal, and I know letting her go could help me find Vyper. She is rumored to be the best when it comes to finding her marks. The woman is mysterious. No one knows who she is or where she came from, but her reputation for being a killer is known by all in the underground of New Orleans.

"I want a man on her, but he needs to know how dangerous and stealthy she is," I order, reaching for the glass of whiskey I'd left when word had come through from my bartender that the woman was snooping around my club. I toss back the remainder and look up at Cyrus to see him staring at me with an odd expression. "What?"

"She called you "Jax"," he states, looking confused.

"She's also a female," I remind him.

"Noted." He nods, straightening his jacket. "I'll have Roman follow her."

With that, Cyrus leaves my office, closing the door with a soft click. I turn around and hit the button on the wall to open the curtains behind my desk. Below is the club, and I watch as Ms. Rayne makes her way to the exit. She turns to the right and disappears from my view. My eyes catch Roman as he tosses his jacket and tie to Alex at the door. It doesn't take long before my guard is out the door and hot on her trail.

Vyper has done the worst thing imaginable, and I will find him and make him disappear for good. No one hurts a female under my watch, and they all know the rules to being one of my employees.

Giggling from the hallway is my only warning before two of my waitresses knock on the door, opening it without my permission. Any other time, I'd welcome them into my office, closing the curtains and locking the door for a little time to blow off steam, but as soon as they enter, I point to the door. "Out!"

Marcy, one of the waitresses, looks at me in shock and I raise my brow. She's always the first one to bring me drinks or volunteer to work when we have private parties.

"Is there a problem?" I ask, narrowing my eyes.

"No sir," she replies. She looks at me for a moment, and I see anger in her eyes, but before I can reply, she scurries out the door.

Cyrus returns with his phone to his ear, casting a glance at the waitresses as they leave in a hurry. He raises a brow at me, but I shake my head, silently telling him that I'm just not in the mood. My mind is filled with thoughts of the huntress and where she is heading.

"Roman said she is just walking the Quarter," he reports, taking a seat in front of my desk. The rope is still on the floor, and he leans over to pick it up. "She's good. I had that knot as tight as I could make it."

Cyrus looks impressed as he coils it up and shoves it in his pocket. Apparently, being a boy scout in his younger years taught him many skills that he could use working for me. Morgan bested him, and I swear I see respect in his eyes as he crosses his ankles.

"What do we know about her?" I inquire, pressing the button to close the curtains behind my desk. From below, the customers have no idea there are windows above them, but I want it that way. Checking in on my business is mandatory, and sometimes being in the crowd is a bad idea.

"Not much," he answers. "She showed up in the Quarter about three years ago, but no one knows where she lives."

"She's hiding from something," I muse.

"Or someone," he adds.

"I want you to find out everything about her," I order, ticking things off on my fingers. "Address, social security number, her mother and father's names, anything you can find."

"I can do that," he says with a grin, loving the task. Cyrus is a genius when it comes to finding information. "What about the shipment coming in tomorrow?"

"The ship will be at the docks by noon," I reply, thumbing through a stack of papers on my desk, pulling out the sheet he'll need to turn over to our guy.

"Which warehouse?" he asks.

"The one in Hammond," I reply.

"Got it." He nods, making a note in his phone. Thankfully, all of our merchandise is clean this time. Being one hundred percent legal is a task in itself, but I need to stay ahead of the authorities. We've been on the watch list for far too long.

"I'm going to bed." I stand and stretch.

"You staying here or going to your home?" he asks.

"Here," I yawn. "I need to be close in case Vyper decides to come back."

"Got it, boss." Cyrus stands and shakes my hand. "I'll take care of everything and leave a report by your door if anything happens while you're asleep."

I nod, dismissing my man, and make my way to the door to my apartment. The stairs lead to my third-floor apartment, and it spans the entire building. I close and lock the door behind me, making my way over to the bar to pour myself a scotch. As I look out the window into the Quarter, I wonder where she is and if she knows where he is hiding.

Chapter 8
Morgan

That asshole has one of his goons following me. I turn onto Royal Street and slip inside a gift shop, pretending to look at some touristy shirts with the city's name on them while I wait for the men to pass. Jackson Pace is adamant about finding my mark before I do, and I'm going to make sure that Vyper is dead before that happens. The owner of the store eyes me suspiciously but doesn't approach.

It takes another few minutes before I leave the building, hoping the guy has given up. I grit my teeth and head the opposite direction when I see another man in a suit hiding around the corner. It's well after dark, and the city is still hot and humid. I feel sweat trickle down my chest, disappearing into my shirt. My feet are starting to ache from wearing my boots, but I can't let that slow me down.

I luck out when I spot a taxi waiting on the corner. Once inside, I tell the driver, "Drive me around until I tell you to stop." The young Haitian man nods and speeds off. As soon as we are out of the Quarter, I sit back in my seat and relax slightly. I need a few minutes to think.

"Just keep driving away from the Quarter," I tell him when he looks in the rearview mirror as if he's waiting for me to give him an address. For good measure, I drop a fifty dollar bill over the seat to shut him up.

"I take you wherever, Ms. Lady," he promises as he assesses me once more from his rearview mirror.

"Thank you," I reply and smile softly. I don't know this guy, and I don't know if he might be working for Jackson Pace. I know I'm being paranoid, but in my business, I have to be cautious. One wrong move could mean my life is over, or I could be caught by the scum I hunt. If that were to ever happen, I'm sure my punishment would be just as bad as what the women I am out here fighting for have been through.

I watch as the meter ticks closer and closer to forty dollars. It's been a good twenty minutes since I jumped in the cab, but I hand him another fifty and say, "When we get close to that, take me to this address." I ramble off the address for the building two blocks from my own. I still don't know who all Jackson Pace has in his pocket. Word travels fast around the Quarter, and I know he's going to be keeping an eye on me.

The driver pulls up to the curb right as the cab rate hits the ninety dollar mark, and I toss him a hundred dollar bill for a tip and make a quick escape from the backseat. He doesn't try to talk to me, and I'm perfectly fine with that. I'm not here to make friends. I enjoy my isolation and my job.

It's been three years since I arrived in this eccentric town, finding refuge amongst this strange, and sometimes unexplainable, city after roaming all over the place, looking to find a little spot where I could hide in plain sight.

My past is my own pain. Once upon a time, I was a young woman planning a future with a husband, kids, the white picket fence…all of it, but one night when I was seventeen changed my life. It's been seven years since the night I was raped, beaten, and left for dead by my father's friend who was also the vice president of a very dangerous biker gang in Portland.

A horn honks up the street, bringing me back from my memories. Like a bad case of post-traumatic stress disorder, my body tightens in preparation for a fight…the need to defend myself, but thankfully, the car passes without slowing.

I have my key in hand as I approach my building, sliding the metal into the lock, turning it as soon it connects, and enjoying the satisfying click of the lock disengaging. My eyes make a sweep of the street as I close the gate and make quick work of climbing the stairs to my apartment above.

As soon as I open my door, I listen for any sounds as I look at the small piece of wrapping paper from a stick of gum that I placed on the carpet before I left earlier. If anyone entered my apartment, they'd step on it, thinking it was nothing more than a discarded piece of trash. To me, it's a security measure. There is no way a person could enter without stepping on it. I breathe a sigh of relief when I see that it has been untouched. Leaning over, I pick it up and place it on the table next to the door and make my way into the kitchen to turn the light on over my small table.

My wrist is a little raw from the rope that Jackson Pace's men had bound me with when I was captured, and I rub at it absently as I mull over the information I'd learned while in the bowels of Club Phoenix.

Jackson is obviously very skilled in his control over his business, and I was surprised when I found out he wasn't hiding Vyper. It also concerns me that the guy I'm looking for has gone missing.

A message lights up my phone, and it's from an unknown sender. Most of the initial contacts from families come up as unknown, because of the secrecy of what I do. From the nature of the text, my time waiting to capture Vyper will be spent working for other people in need.

I need help finding my mother.

I stand from my uncomfortable couch and head to my bedroom and the hidden safe in the wall behind my dresser. It houses all of my weapons and the documents to keep my real identity hidden. I find what I need and put the phone to my ear. When a young woman's voice cracks on the other end, I lock down my emotions.

"Tell me everything you know," I demand. Once I have the information, I leave my apartment and go hunting in the city.

Chapter 9
Jackson

Cyrus wakes me at three in the morning. Morgan Rayne has been found, but she isn't at home. "Morgan rescued a woman from a crack house, and she was beat up pretty badly by the woman's pimp. She's refusing medical services."

"Where is she?" I bark, dressing in my ripped-up jeans. I grab a black cotton shirt and pull it over my head while I wait for my right-hand man to show me the photos on his phone.

"Roman followed her," Cyrus informs me. "He lost her for a few hours, and that's all it took for Ms. Rayne to get into a mess."

"Did she save the woman?" I ask.

"Yeah," Cyrus chuckles, but composes himself when I raise a brow in his direction. "Ms.

Rayne left him in quite some pain, sir. Here, I have photos."

I cringe when Cyrus hands me the photos Roman texted him. The pimp's face looks like he'd been jumped by a gang. His shoulder is bleeding from a bullet wound, and he's doubled over as he holds on to his junk like he'd been kicked by a horse.

Anger burns through my veins when I come to the pictures of Morgan. One of her eyes is swollen shut and she has blood trailing out of her mouth. Her knuckles are covered in blood, but I'm not sure if the red stain on her beautiful skin belongs to her or the pimp.

"Get her here," I order, trying to calm my shaking hands while I reach for my own phone. "I'll have my physician check her out."

"Yes, sir," Cyrus replies and disappears out the door, closing it softly behind him.

Chapter 10
Morgan

"Ow," I protest as the doctor presses a cotton ball to the cut over my eye. "I'm fine, and it wouldn't hurt if you'd quit touching it!"

"Morgan, let the physician examine you," Jackson scolds as he leans against the wall with his ankle crossed over the other one. He's not wearing any shoes, like he was in a hurry to come to the room when I arrived.

"Excuse me? I don't need to be looked at by a doctor," I scoff, pushing the doc's hand away so I can glare at the man who forced me back into his club. "No one tells me what to do."

"You're in my home," he growls. "You will do as I tell you."

"I'm done here," I snap and stand up from the stool at the bar in his home above the club. The music has died down, but the doors are not closed. This is New Orleans, after all. Bars are open twenty-four hours a day.

"Sit," he orders. Blood creeps up his neck, and I don't even have to guess that he is angry. His darkening green eyes are another sign. I flop down on the stool and cross my arms over my chest, pinning him with a hard glare as he nods for the doctor to resume checking me out.

"I'm used to getting a few bumps and bruises," I say as I roll my eyes. "You are over-reacting."

I was surprised to see one of his men come to my rescue at the pimp's house. I'd done what I was paid to do; get the woman out and teach the man a lesson. What I didn't expect was the woman to distract me by begging to let her stay. She was under the pimp's control, and the drugs he kept pumped in her system overpowered her sense of reasoning. She'd been missing from her family for three months, and they were desperate to save her.

"I don't think you have any broken bones in your face, but you will need to keep ice on that eye for at least another hour." The doctor gathers his supplies in a little black bag and turns toward Jackson, accepting an envelope before walking out the door.

"What happened?" Jackson asks, ignoring my statement earlier. His man, Roman, was standing by the door looking as pissed off as a wet cat. The large man was dressed in a black suit and tie with a white button-down shirt. His hair was as black as night and his eyes were blue like expensive sapphires.

"The woman grabbed my arm, begging me to stop hitting her pimp," I snarl, looking over at Jackson's employee. "Roman busted through the door about the time the pimp returned the favor." I point at my eye.

"Did you finish him?" Jackson inquires, looking over at Roman for answers. When Roman inclines his head toward where I'm sitting, Jackson levels his stare back on me to await my answer.

"I shot him, but I didn't kill him."

"Good," he says, clasping his hands behind his back. "Roman, did you assist her?"

"No, sir," Roman answers, and I notice a bit of respect in his gaze. "She did it all on her own. I was ready to kill the son of a bitch, but Ms. Rayne is very thorough in her jobs."

"Why didn't you kill him?" Jackson asks,

making me feel very uncomfortable talking about my day job.

"The details of what I do are none of your business," I growl. "While I appreciate your man getting me out of there, that doesn't give you permission to ask me questions about my clients."

"I beg to differ, Ms. Rayne," he says, narrowing his eyes. One minute, he's standing in front of me, and the next, he's in my face. I can taste his unique scent on my tongue, and I close my eyes for a second to get my wits about me again before he starts to speak. "I just paid for the female you saved to go into extensive treatment for her drug addiction and to be seen by my physician to ensure she comes out of it healthy. That alone gives me permission to know what the fuck you are up to."

My jaw tenses with his demands. I didn't lie when I said to him that I don't like being told what to do. I don't know this man, and his sudden worry for me feels foreign. His sexiness and power may scare other women, but I am not like them. The danger in his eyes mesmerizes me.

"No," I reply, simple and to the point. I can feel his hot breath on my cheek as I turn my head slightly. He's so close I can feel his power, and my body responds.

"If you don't tell me, I cannot keep you from being killed by Vyper," he says through gritted teeth. I inhale and immediately curse at myself. He smells like an all-powerful male, and I find the scent more appealing than I should. "Your life was dangerous before, but I promise you this, Ms. Rayne...Vyper will kill you to stay alive. I'm going to try to keep him from getting to you, but you have to work with me, too."

"He's mine," I reply.

"How much is the family paying you to kill him?" he blurts out. Jackson's eyes keep darkening, and I find myself mesmerized by his anger. I don't know why I test the beast, but I do.

"I don't know what you're talking about," I whisper.

"Roman, leave us," Jackson says without looking over his shoulder. Our eyes are locked in a battle of wills when I hear his guard leave the room. His lip piercing rolls with his agitation, and I want to take the metal between my teeth. I shake that thought from my head but never break my stare.

"You are playing with fire, Morgan," he says, his eyes breaking away to trace the contours of my face...my lips. I automatically swipe my bottom one with my tongue to moisten where it's suddenly gone bone dry.

"What do you know about me?" I taunt, hoping to dig deeper into what he knows.

"You are called 'The Huntress' in the underground," he begins. "You only go after men who've harmed women in the worst ways. You showed up in New Orleans about three years ago, and no one knows where you came from. Do I need to continue?"

"No," I answer, moving to slide off the stool. Jackson turns around and walks over to the small bar built into the wall to pour himself a drink. It's four in the morning, but he seems to not care much for that as he tosses it back, slamming the glass down on the tile.

"Why?" he pauses to shake his head, "I want to know why you do what you do."

"That is a secret I will take to my grave," I answer.

"You've covered your past very well, Morgan."

"Sometimes you have to bury your past." I walk over to his bar and grab a clean glass, pouring myself a shot of expensive tequila I find in the cabinet, not caring to ask for permission. I make myself a double shot and set my glass next to his after knocking back the liquid. "Can I go home now, or are you going to tell me more about myself that I already know?"

Chapter 11
Jackson

I don't know if I want to strangle or kiss this woman. She's tough as nails, and I'm finding myself more protective of her by the second. The swollen black eye will haunt me for nights to come.

"I want to hire you," I offer. Even though I know she's going to deny me, I map out a plan in my head. Morgan is smart enough to find him. However, I doubt she is able enough to bring Vyper down the way she plans.

"Hire me?" she laughs.

"Yes," I answer, motioning for her to take a seat on my couch. She slips into the corner on the furthest end from where I have taken a seat in my high back chair. "I want to hire you to help me find Vyper."

"I've been hired by the girl's family."

"I will pay you double what they are offering if you bring him to me alive," I press. If I can't get her to tell me what she knows, maybe I can pay her for her information.

"I don't do this for the money," she says sadly, looking away from me to stare at the floor. "I do it for the women."

Morgan removes the tie from her hair and puts it on her wrist, immediately fidgeting with the band. She pops it several times against her skin, and I can tell she's nervous. She abruptly stops when she notices me staring at her tic.

"Does that calm you?" I ask, lowering my voice.

"Yes," she breathes.

"What happened to you?" I lean forward and rest my elbows on the tops of my knees to look more relaxed, but Morgan stiffens and jumps to her feet. She presses her hand to her swollen eye and curses. I'm immediately in front of her. "Morgan, shhh, sit down and relax."

"I'm tired." She blows out a harsh breath. "Can I go home?"

"You shouldn't be alone. You took a pretty hard hit to that eye," I remind her. "Please, be my guest. I have a spare room with a bathroom. You are welcome to stay here."

Morgan looks at me, judging my features to see if I'm up to no good. She's smart and cunning. Either she is looking for something good in me to make her feel safe, or she's going to bolt as soon as I close my eyes.

"The door locks so you can feel safe," I add.

"Okay, fine." She relaxes. "I'll stay."

"I'll show you to your room, and you can stay as long as you need," I tell her, holding my hand out to the left to indicate she should go ahead of me. The spare room is on the other side of my apartment from my own room. In the middle is a kitchen that opens to the sitting area we are in now. It's simple and provides what I need when I stay in the city.

I walk her to the door, and her shoulder brushes my chest as I lean past her to push it open wide. I haven't been in this room since I had it designed. The queen size bed sits under the floor to ceiling window, and the light blue colors and fluffy bedding looks inviting.

"Goodnight, Jax," she yawns. We are close…so close I could press my lips to hers, but I refrain. Morgan Rayne has a hard shell, and I want to slowly unravel the mystery behind who she really is.

"Goodnight, Ms. Rayne." I nod and walk away, not entering my room until I hear the lock engage on her door. She's safe here, and I place a call to my men to make sure she is protected while I sleep.

Chapter 12
Morgan

The moment I wake up, I know I am not home. I pull the plush comforter over my body and nestle back into the bed that has to be made from the most expensive material Jackson Pace can afford. For once, I don't have a spring in my side from my old couch.

I could have this luxury if I use the money I earn from the families, but I can't bring myself to do it. My conscious won't even allow it.

I did nothing more than remove my shoes before I fell asleep early that morning in Jackson Pace's apartment. Closing my eyes, I listen for movement and breathe a sigh of relief when I hear none. I'm shocked when I look at the clock and the time says it's well past five in the evening. I haven't slept that long in ages.

My shoes are where I left them when I finally emerge from beneath the covers. Checking my phone, I have no messages. My eye throbs from the punch I took at the pimp's house, but I ignore it and get out of bed. I use the restroom and wash my face with cold water. When I look in the mirror, I see a tired woman staring back at me. She looks like she's aged thirty years in the last seven.

"It doesn't matter," I whisper to my reflection and shake my head. I can't think of myself right now. I have a job to do.

Jackson was overly worried for my safety, and his man, Roman, had insisted I return with him to Club Phoenix to be looked at by their doctor. I wouldn't admit to them, but I was glad Roman was there to help me with the woman. She was so far gone in her addiction that she refused treatment. Thankfully, Jackson knew someone who could force her into a program without the law getting involved. The pimp is still alive for all I know. Roman had been so angry, I wouldn't put it past that man to return and take the pimp out himself.

"Ms. Rayne," Roman says as I exit the bedroom. I nod and head for the door, hoping he will just let me pass. I don't want to be here any longer than necessary. "Mr. Pace would like to see you before you leave today."

"And where is Mr. Pace?" I ask, gritting my teeth. I don't want to see him anymore than I have to. That man stirs a feeling inside me I don't want awakened while I'm on the hunt. It's important that I focus on the job that needs to be done.

"In his office," Roman says, standing from his seat at the bar. He folds the paper neatly and straightens his jacket. "I'll walk you down."

The guard is as big as all the others who work for Jackson. However, Roman doesn't have massive amounts of tattoos on his hands or neck like his coworkers. He looks like he's been plucked off a health magazine for men. His hair is short to his head and black as night. I detect a slight foreign accent, but I cannot place it. His arms are three times the size of my thighs, and I know he's not someone I would want to piss off from the permanent scowl on his face.

"Thank you for showing up last night," I say as a peace offering. It takes a lot for me to accept help, but the pimp was ruthless. If it wasn't for Roman's distraction, I probably would've been in much worse shape. This isn't the first time I have been struck by a mark, and it probably won't be the last.

"What you do is dangerous," he grunts, and opens the door to exit Jackson's apartment. There is a set of stairs at the landing, and I follow him down to the next floor, turning right down a short hallway.

As we walk, I see a door to my left. It is ajar, and I hear voices of several men. I don't slow as I pass, but I do get a good glimpse at a round table that holds five men and a dealer. All of them are dressed in suits, and the fresh scent of cigar smoke filters across my nose as I pass. The sound of poker chips reaches my ears as someone pushes the door closed.

"I do what I must, damn the consequences." Roman nods as if he accepts my answer and opens the door to the office. Jackson is on the phone, pacing a hole in his carpet as he looks out over the bar. I take a seat in front of his desk and wait until he hangs up.

"You wanted to see me before I left?" I ask. I should be a smartass and mention the illegal gambling just down the hall, but I don't. It's none of my business.

"Did you think any more about my offer of employment?"

"I don't do well with authority, Jax," I shrug. "I work alone."

"I don't think what I'm asking of you permits

you to be put on my payroll, Morgan," he remarks. He's dressed in jeans and a light gray cotton shirt. When he turns slightly to the right, I see more ink at his collarbone as he makes himself comfortable. He rolls the piercing in his lip twice before he continues. "It's safer for you if you are working for me."

"How so?"

"I have certain…contracts with people in this city," he replies, leaning back in his chair. He steeples his fingers in front of his face, tapping them on his full lips. "I will give you a list of these people, they know things. They will talk when asked."

"So, you have eyes all over the city?" I ask, already knowing the answer to my own question.

"Yes," he answers simply, looking over my shoulder. "Thank you, Roman."

Roman slides out the door, pulling it closed with a soft click. I know Jackson's men are always close. I learned that the first time I was here. This man is deadly, and under a lot of protection.

"If I do work for you," I begin, but hold up my hand when he starts to talk. "I mean, *if* I decide to help you find Vyper, I want assurance that I am the one to take him out."

"I cannot do that," Jackson shakes his head as if he's dislodging a bad memory, "I'm paying you to find him. When you do, you tell me where he is, and my men will bring him to me. He knows the rules when it comes to pledging himself to me, and he broke that trust."

"If I'm not going to be able to finish my job," I shrug, "then I will go out on my own."

My phone rings from my pocket, and I ignore his reply as I answer. It's another request, and I take a deep breath as the mother on the other end tells me about the man who has been abusive to her daughter for the past six months. He's rumored to be coming to the family home today despite the restraining order.

"Give me an address," I reply, standing up to grab a pen and sticky note from Jackson's desk. I also ignore his raised brow at my brashness. *I'm not a lady, Mr. Pace. I hate to disappoint you.* "I'll be there in twenty minutes."

"Where is this one?" Jackson inquires. I stare at him for a moment, calculating how much I should tell him. This request is pretty tame compared to the others. I lock down and press my lips together. I don't want anyone to know what I'm doing out in this city. The less people that know, the better. "I know what you do, Morgan. You need to trust me."

"The last man I trusted used that against me," I say with a glare. Shaking my head, I turn to leave but Jackson's hands slapping the top of his desk has me turning around. His eyes have darkened, and he's pissed.

"Who hurt you?" His demand is spoken with so much authority, I feel like he is trying to pull the words from my tongue. I have to resist his power, but it's hard.

"Not your business." I slash my hand through the air and turn to leave. I don't need to tell him what happened to me, because I cannot be found. I hide for a reason.

"Tell me where you are going," he demands.

"The mother needs someone there when the boyfriend shows up despite the restraining order she has on him," I offer after a heavy sigh.

"Have Roman go with you," Jackson says, as if his word is final.

"I don't need him," I say. "I don't need help."

"Morgan," he warns, but I ignore him and leave his office. None of his men try to stop me as I take the stairs down to the bar floor, opening the door I'd been standing by when I was originally taken up to his office, bound and blindfolded.

Out on the street, tourists look at me with wide eyes. The swelling around my eye has gone down enough for me to be able to see clearly through it, but the bruise stands out like a bright beacon. I stop by my place and change clothes. I grab a pair of sunglasses and my Glock, hiding it in a holster at my side. Once I double check the locks on my doors, I am off to meet the female at her home.

Chapter 13
Jackson

"Bring the car around back," I bark into the phone and reach into my desk. I palm my gun and grab a holster to hide the weapon at my back. Cyrus enters the office as I'm grabbing my phone from the desk. "Is Roman following her?"

"She's at her apartment," Cyrus informs me with a frown.

"Why has she stopped there?" This little hitwoman has taken up my every thought, and the concern I have for her is eating me alive. I remembered her comment in my office, and heat boils in my veins as I try to quickly decipher what she meant. *The last man I trusted used that against me.*

"You're not going to like where she lives," Cyrus answers.

The last man I trusted used that against me.
Her voice echoes through my head with those words.
They make my heart physically hurt.

"Where?"

He tells me the cross streets in the Quarter,
and I curse out loud, walking toward the door. I will
deal with her living arrangements when I make sure
she doesn't end up shot by this man who obviously
cannot accept the court-ordered restraining order the
woman has out on him.

My driver, Keon, is standing by the car,
holding the door open as I walk at a fast pace toward
the vehicle. "Roman has given me the location."

"I am armed," I growl as I slide into my seat,
letting my man know I don't need his protection
should something go down. Keon closes the door and
hurries into the driver's seat, leaving the parking
garage behind the bar as the sun is setting over the
city. She's out there in the dark and my anxiety
heightens. What if the call she got was a hoax by
Vyper to get her alone?

The last man I trusted used that against me. I
shake my head to try to dislodge her voice. I'm
fascinated by her, and the more I think about the
huntress, the more I want to know about her. I close
my eyes and I see her. When I let my guard down, I

hear her hardened voice in my head, and I wonder what she'd sound like if she wasn't tortured and out for vengeance.

I try to fight the resolve in my mind, but it's no use, Morgan will be protected by me because I cannot let her be taken by the man she's looking for.

No one knows just how dangerous Vyper can be. Only my men and I have knowledge of the things he has done, and how much he gets off on the pleasure of his specialty. The man is the devil reincarnated. It only took six months before I started questioning him about just how dangerous he really was. It took another three months before the news came of a woman he'd left in an abandoned hotel just outside of the Quarter. By the time the news reached me, he'd hurt the woman whose family hired Morgan Rayne. After that, Vyper disappeared. I've tried looking for him in all of his usual haunts, but he's gone. No one has heard from him. None of my contacts have seen him in the city.

"She's in her car," Keon says after hanging up his phone. I'm sure Roman is hot on her heels. "It looks like she's heading toward the fairgrounds."

"Go," I tell him, leaning back in my seat. "When we get close, park down the street."

We are there within five minutes after Roman

arrives. Keon cuts the lights and pulls in behind my other guard. I kill the interior lights as I open the door and walk up to slide into the passenger seat of Roman's vehicle.

"She's tough," Roman says, pointing out her small car and the house she entered.

"She's playing roulette with her life." I squeeze my fists where they're resting on the tops of my knees. I want to rush into that home and take her out of there, but I know that it would probably get me a black eye from the huntress herself. "Has any information on her past been found?"

"None," Roman replies, tapping his fingers on the steering wheel. "I have a feeling her name is actually an alias."

The last man I trusted used that against me.

"So, you think Morgan Rayne isn't even her name?" I ask, looking over at him and seeing concern on the man's face. My hard-as-stone bodyguard is showing a sign of weakness for her, and it surprises me. None of my men have ever slipped, and the jealous side of me wants to know what feelings Roman has for her.

"I sense the question you're not asking, Jackson," Roman begins, swiveling his head so he is looking me dead in the eye. "Morgan, if that's even her name, reminds me of Vera."

My guard closes his eyes and releases a deep breath before turning back to watch the house up ahead. I don't even need to ask any further into his statement. Vera was his sister. She'd been well on her way to becoming a female MMA fighter, and one night when she was leaving the gym, she was gunned down by a gang member in the city. I made sure the man was found and punished for his crimes before the law could arrest him.

The case was closed within forty-eight hours.

"There's a car pulling in down the street," Roman announces, pointing at an old, white Cadillac. We watch as a man exits and reaches inside the car. I can't make out what he grabs, but Roman immediately knows. "He's got a gun."

"Fuck." I grab for the door handle, but Roman reaches out to stop me.

"You are not safe in this area, Jackson. Stay here, I will go," he pleads.

"My safety isn't important," I bellow, pushing his hand away. "Morgan's is."

Roman curses but doesn't stop me when I step out of his car, closing the door softly. We take to the sidewalk on the opposite side of the street, using the cover of the cars parked on the road as we follow him.

"Damn it, Morgan." I grit my teeth and lower myself behind a sedan.

She's standing on the porch of the home, her feet are shoulder-width apart, and she looks pissed. The man stops at the bottom of the stairs, and we are close enough to hear the anger in his voice.

"I want my wife!" he barks.

"Terrance." Morgan shakes her head, holding her ground. "There is a restraining order against you. From the papers, you are already too close to Benita."

"Fuck you, bitch," he spits out. I want to end him. Hearing a man use that tone with her sends my anger into dangerous territory. If Ms. Rayne doesn't kill him, I will make sure I bloody my own hands to teach him a lesson.

"Turn around and go home," Morgan replies, pointing up the road to where his car is parked. "We can do this the easy way, or we can do this the hard way. Benita isn't going to see you tonight. You can talk to her in court tomorrow at your divorce hearing."

"What are *you* going to do about it?" he sneers. I can see his head slowly move up and down like he's sizing her up. Roman removes his gun from the shoulder holster beneath his jacket. I mimic him by pulling mine from the one at my back.

"If he touches her, I'm taking the shot," Roman whispers. "You get her out, and I'll deal with the rest. Go straight home." I do nothing more than nod and watch the scene in front of me.

Morgan takes one step down the stairs, putting herself closer to this asshole. Blood pumps through my veins, and I want to shoot this fucker myself. There is no one around to see us, and I'm about ready to run at her to take her away from this guy.

"I am here as protection for Benita Jones," she states, standing her ground. "I am trained in three different martial arts, and I am carrying a weapon. So, I'd advise you to do as you're told and turn around. Leave her alone."

"You don't scare me," he chuckles. Morgan raises a brow as if he's bluffing. I want to scream at her to run, because I know he's serious. Her shoulders square, and I know she's just as angry and on edge as I am.

"There is an order of protection. You must abide by that, because if you don't, you will be in serious trouble, and you will never see your children again, Terrance. Don't make this hard on yourself."

Damn, there are children involved. I see Roman start to stand, but he sinks back into his position next to me when Terrance's shoulders slump. The man starts to leave, turning his back on Morgan. She doesn't leave her spot on the second step, her eyes narrowing as if she knows he isn't done.

My heart begins to thrum at a faster pace as the scene in front of me plays out in slow motion. Terrance reaches into the front of his jeans and removes a gun. I swear I can hear the safety release from across the street when he expertly palms the weapon. Roman curses as he takes off at a dead run.

Morgan drops to a crouch as the man raises his weapon. She is quick…almost too quick. I've never even seen my men move like she does. Like some paranormal creature with super speed on their side, she launches herself as the gun discharges. Her body jolts and Terrance pushes her away, knocking her head against the concrete pathway.

"*Morgan!*" I'm on Roman's heels, running as fast as I can to reach her. My legs feel as if they are trudging through swamp mud. I know I'm moving toward her, but the distance isn't closing between us like it should.

"You motherfucker!" I hear her shout when my foot hits the curb. She's only feet away from me, and I say a prayer to whatever god is out there to hear my plea that she isn't hurt. Rage burns through my veins, and my anger boils to a point that the monster inside me rears his head when Roman grabs her, rolling her small body over…and all I see is blood.

"Morgan!" I yell.

"I'm fine," she pants. "He shot me in the fucking arm and grazed me."

My hands tear at her shirt, ripping the sleeve. I immediately remove the cotton shirt I'm wearing and press it to her wound. "I've got you."

"Fuck, my head hurts," she moans, and presses the palm of her hand to her temple.

"You hit your head pretty hard." I'm so mad right now. This man hurt her with no remorse…no second thought to it. No wonder the woman has a restraining order out on the guy. When I look up toward the house, I see two women standing at the window beside the door. I ignore them, because they are safe and, thankfully, not coming out to see what the hell is going on in their yard.

"What are you doing here?" she asks, narrowing her eyes. She's pissed that I followed her, but I don't really want to talk to her right now. "You're not supposed to be here!"

The last man I trusted used that against me. I want to prove my worth to her and ensure she can trust someone…me.

Out of the corner of my eye, Roman kicks the gun from Terrance's hand and nails him in the jaw with his fist. I don't even need to watch him to know Roman is giving the man everything he deserves, and I hope my man kills the bastard.

"Jackson," she calls out, but I keep my head turned away from her to make sure Roman has the man in check. "Jackson? Jax!"

"I really don't think it's a great idea to talk to me right now, Morgan," I warn, pressing my shirt to her arm a little tighter. Blood is oozing slowly from the wound, and I need to get her to my doctor to have it looked at.

"You're making a big deal out of this," she huffs.

With my free hand, I dig my phone out of my pocket and call Cyrus. "Morgan's been shot. We have the guy, but I need transport and the doc to meet me at my home…not the club."

I don't need to tell him where I am. Cyrus will be here within minutes, and I hope he gets here before someone calls the cops. Thankfully, we are in a neighborhood where gunshots on any given night is as common as it gets.

I turn back to Morgan, and she's laying beneath me with wide, blue eyes. There are no tears in them, but I know she must be in pain. I've never met a woman as tough as her, and again, she intrigues me.

"Do you hurt?" That's all I can get out at the moment. I'm still so fucking angry at her, Terrance, and the entire situation.

"Why are you following me?" she asks.

"I really don't fucking know," I growl.

The last man I trusted used that against me. That is the reason, my little huntress. Seeing her laying on the ground sends my protective instincts into high gear. I want that man dead!

"I'm fine, Jackson," she says, her voice softer. "Can you let me sit up?"

"No," I bark, placing my hand on her shoulder to keep her still. She struggles for a moment, but I don't ease up on my hold. "Help is coming. I want to make sure that bullet didn't do any damage."

"Jesus, Jackson!" she hollers. "Let me get the fuck off the ground."

"No," I reply.

Thankfully, a black SUV arrives, and Cyrus rushes out. A second later, another one arrives and two of my men pile out. Terrance is unconscious when Roman and the two other men pick him up, dragging his worthless ass out to the vehicle, tossing him inside.

"Hey, Morgan," Cyrus says, kneeling down next to me. "Let me take a look."

"Are you a doctor?" she scoffs, narrowing her eyes.

"No, but I do have some medical training," he replies, waiting for me to remove my hand from her arm where I have my shirt pressing against her wound. It worries me the amount of blood that is coming from the wound. He lifts the shirt but doesn't show any emotion that would tell me anything about the condition of her wound. "We definitely need to have it sewn up."

"Where are you taking me?"

"Back to the doc," Cyrus replies, holding his hand on the shirt. I slide my arm behind her shoulder, using the other to hook under her knees. When I lift her, she grunts a little and I freeze, worrying I have hurt her, but when she starts cursing at me again, I ignore her and start walking. We slide into the back of the SUV, and before I know it, Cyrus is heading away from the scene. Roman is still on the porch, talking to the woman who lives there. I assume it's the lady who has the restraining order or her mother.

"Benita is okay?" Morgan asks as she pinches her eyes closed. I'm still holding her as if she is nothing more than a baby in my arms. I just can't let her go at the moment. I shouldn't be this protective of a female, but I am.

"Benita is the woman with the restraining order?" I ask.

"Yes," she replies, sucking in a breath when Cyrus takes a sharp right to take the ramp onto the highway.

"Roman is taking care of everything," I promise. "The woman is safe."

"Thank god," she breathes, looking up at me through her lashes, and the vulnerability in her eyes punches me straight in the chest. "I was handling it by myself."

"So, how many times do you get shot at by these assholes, Morgan?" My question is harsh. I'm so fucking angry right now, I want to kill Terrance with my bare hands and take her across my knee for putting herself in danger.

"Ah, not very often." She shrugs, cursing when the pain in her arm flares. "I'm going to be fine."

"Try to relax," I urge, calming down. "We will be at my house in ten minutes."

"I thought you lived at the bar."

"I have a home outside of the city," I tell her.

"The apartment at the bar is for late nights when I don't feel like going home." Or we have huge parties with our clients, providing whatever they need…legal or otherwise.

"So, you're taking me there?" she asks, looking a little fearful.

"Don't worry, little huntress," I say, tucking a stray lock of her dark hair behind her ear to offer comfort. When she relaxes from my touch, I feel more connected to her than I did when she stepped into my bar looking for my enforcer. "No one will hurt you there."

The last man I trusted used that against me.

Chapter 14
Morgan

We arrive at a mansion outside of the city
about the time I'm hurting more than I want to admit.
It bothers me that I don't know where I am, because I
spent the last twenty minutes laid out in the backseat
of his expensive SUV, bleeding out from the wound
on the outside of my arm several inches above my
elbow.

As soon as we pull up in the circle drive, a
man dressed in a black suit opens one of the double
doors to the front of the house. I'm momentarily
stunned at the magnificence of the outside of the
home. The doors are a dark-stained wood, and the
brick on the home is white. The stark contrast is
beautiful.

"Morgan?" Jackson whispers. It isn't until

then that I realize how weak my body has become since I got shot. "The doctor is inside."

I wait for him to exit the vehicle before I slide to the edge of the seat. The moment my feet hit the ground, I have no strength to hold myself upright. Jackson wraps his arm around my waist and gives me a gentle squeeze. My adrenaline has died down, and with the blood loss and the hit I took to my head, I'm surprised I haven't blacked out yet.

Our eyes lock; his green to my blue. An electric current flows between us as his gaze turns to concern. This man…this dangerous man is showing compassion, and it throws me. I don't do feelings from anyone, and I sense his concern from the way he holds me close to his chest. I still do not trust this man, but at this point, he is all I have. I can't quite walk into the hospital without someone wanting answers; someone meaning the police.

"No hospital, I promise." Jackson whispers against my hair like he's keeping my secret. My mind is hazy, and I cringe when I realize I'm mumbling aloud. "No police either."

Fuck! I need to keep my mouth shut.

Bright lights make me squint when we enter the foyer to the home. There are white tile floors everywhere I can see, and as we walk through the living room that's five times larger than my apartment, I notice several men in suits standing by the back floor-to-ceiling windows. All of them are stoic and unmoving, but their eyes follow us as we enter a hallway.

"Tell me what happened," the doctor I saw before barks as we enter a large bedroom. The covers on the king size bed are already pulled back, and the doctor has set out several instruments on the bedside table. I hear a television somewhere off in the distance but can't make out what is playing.

"Gunshot wound to her left arm." Jackson's voice sounds panicked as he places me on the bed. He hesitates a second as our noses come within inches of each other. I can see it in his eyes. He wants to say something to me, but he doesn't. He steps away and I see he is without a shirt and there is blood on his hands and chest.

"Were you shot?" My voice is gone. I'm so damn thirsty. I want to know if he was hit.

"No," he says as he shakes his head. "This is yours. Doctor Barnes is going to take a look at you."

"Ms. Rayne," the doc starts as he leans over me. "I'm going to be as gentle as I can, but I need to see this arm."

I shift on the bed, turning so he can get a good

look. I still think Jackson is making a big deal about the whole thing. He curses as the doctor makes a disapproving sound in the back of his throat. When he lets me lie back, I catch sight of Jackson's back as he leaves the room. A few seconds later, Roman enters and stands at the door, his hands clasped in front of him like he's on guard duty.

"The bullet did graze you, but it took a lot of meat with it," the doc announces. My eyes haven't left Roman's, and I relax slightly when I see the relief on his face. My eyes swing toward the doc, and immediately they widen when I see him holding a syringe. "I'm going to give you something for the pain."

"No!" I panic. I don't like being sedated. It makes me vulnerable, and I can't do that again. "No!" I yell again, and Roman pushes away from the wall to come to the doctor's side. Both men look like they are going to kill someone.

"Morgan, what is it?" Roman asks.

"No, I can't be sedated," I repeat, pushing the doctor away. "Get away from me!"

"Morgan!" Roman yells as I start to fight.

The fear of sedation grasps my soul and tears it from my body. Wetness splashes against my cheeks, and I realize tears are falling from my eyes. I see the doctor raise a needle to the air after removing the cap. They don't understand. I can't be sedated…I need to get out of here.

My foot connects with Roman's arm, knocking him away. I spin on the bed, coming down hard on my damaged arm, but I use all of my force to get back up before he can grab me. The doctor steps away from the bed as my feet land on solid ground. I crouch low, preparing to fight.

I calculate the distance between where I am and the door. Roman is closer and will be there to block me. I check the windows, but the panes look too thick to break. I need to find another way out.

"Morgan, the windows are bulletproof for Jackson's safety," he begins, holding his hands out in front of him to show me he is unarmed. "You need to let the doc take care of you."

"Jackson?" I ask, wondering where the fuck he is. "Where is he?"

"He's taking care of some business," Roman answers, but I know he's lying.

My panicked mind is screaming for the man who is just as deadly as myself. Why in the hell do I feel so safe with him? Should I feel safe with him? Where is he?

"I want to leave," I beg, my eyes bounce from

the doc to Roman and back again. "I have to get out of here."

"You need to let the doctor patch you up first," Roman pleads. "After that, you can go."

The throbbing from the wound is getting worse, and I can feel the blood trickling down my arm. I take a quick glance and frown. There is a lot of blood, and my arm does need to be stitched. All I need to do is get back to my turf in the Quarter, and I can go to Landry to be sewn up. I've done it before.

"No sedative." I glance at the doc. He's still holding the needle, and I want to kick his hand, too.

Roman starts to move toward me, taking two steps. I drop back into a stance, raising my fists up to my face. Fuck, my arm is killing me. "I don't want to hurt you, Roman."

"What the fuck is going on!" Jackson bellows from the doorway.

Tears fill my eyes as soon as I see him standing there looking like a knight in tattooed armor. He's changed into a ripped-up concert shirt. His tattooed arms flex as he pushes into the room, walking toward me like he's there to either kiss me or kick my ass. I don't move from my spot as he approaches. "What's the problem?"

"No sedation," I growl, looking over at the

doc.

"Why?" he demands.

"I...I can't," I blurt, not giving a reason. I can't even begin to tell him why I have such a fear of being knocked out. Not having control over my body sends such a panic through me, I am blinded by rage. I'll take him out if he gets in my way. "It's best that you just let me leave, because if that doctor comes toward me with that needle, we are going to have big problems, Jax."

"Morgan," he sighs, coming over to stand in front of me. I'm still in defensive mode; my hands are up and I'm ready to fight.

Jackson takes one look at me and immediately turns to the doc and Roman. "Leave the room. Now!" Both men comply, shutting the door tight on their way out.

"Morgan," he coos, taking my hands into his. I relax slightly when his thumbs rub gentle circles over the tops of my knuckles. "We need to give you something so he can close the wound on your arm. Now, tell me why you are scared."

"I'm *not* scared," I growl, standing upright. God, he smells so good. I think he took a shower in another room, and his scent distracts me enough, I don't pull away when Jackson tugs me closer to his chest.

"I just witnessed a panic attack," he says, still holding my fists, but not my wrists. It doesn't escape me that his touch is calculated to ease me. I'm okay with that, because I still have a way out if I feel cornered. "You have to talk to me."

"I don't even know you," I breathe, looking into his eyes. I find comfort there again, but this time, it doesn't unnerve me. It relaxes me.

"Tell me what's wrong so that I may fix it," he continues.

"Being sedated takes my control away." I swallow, pausing to find the connection in his eyes again. "The last time I was sedated, things happened."

"What things?"

"The things that made me who I am," I hedge. "Just believe me, please. I cannot be put under. I will fight you, the doctor, and Roman."

"I'm certain he can give you a local pain reliever. Will that be okay?" he asks.

"Yes," I nod, stepping away from him. He's too close, and I don't trust myself around him.

"Take a seat on the bed, and I will fetch the doctor for you," he commands. I obey and take my seat, but I don't lay back. I have to be upright while he is gone. I don't know if anyone is going to come in and knock me out.

Jackson returns with the doctor, and I see that he's discarded the sedative. I relax a little more as Jackson speaks softly to the doctor. Roman is nowhere to be found, and I immediately feel sorry for fighting him.

"I'm going to numb the area, Morgan," the doc says as he removes a fresh needle from his bag. "I'll give you a few shots, then leave you alone for a bit to give the medicine a chance to work. After that, I will stitch the wound, and I will leave you with some antibiotics. Is that okay?"

"It's fine," I say, my teeth clenching tight.

"I'm not leaving your side," Jackson says as he sits next to me on the bed. His hand lands on my right hand, and it's only then that I realize I've been picking at the extra hair tie on my wrist. The popping sound of the band against my skin registers, and I stop, pulling my hand away from his.

Doctor Barnes injects me in several places, and I don't even flinch. That pain is nothing compared to being shot. He caps the needle and sets it on the bedside table before quietly leaving. I wait for the feel of the medicine to start working, hoping they didn't trick me and sedate me anyway.

"He's not going to trick you," Jackson

guesses, placing a hand on my knee. "There is a bathroom attached to this room. It has all of the supplies you need to clean up afterward. If there is something you need, and I don't have it, I will get it for you."

"I think you are making a big deal over nothing," I finally say after a few moments of silence. "I can handle myself."

"What would you have done if I wasn't there tonight?" Jackson Pace is angry, and I can almost feel the wrath coming from his body.

"I have a friend who has patched me up more times than I can count," I admit.

"Hmm," he hums, and I think he's jealous.

"Thank you for this, but I have to leave afterward," I announce. "Can Roman drop me off in the Quarter?"

"No, you're staying here tonight." He frowns, shaking his head slightly. "I don't want you going back to that crappy apartment over the restaurant."

"I knew you'd have eyes all over the place to watch me," I snarl. "I don't know where Vyper is. Why don't you believe me?"

"Right now, this has nothing to do with Vyper," he snaps, leaning over so that we were inches apart. "I want you to tell me what happened to you to make you so fucking scared of being knocked out."

"Ah," I shake my head, "I don't tell my secrets to anyone...not even you, Jax."

His fingers tighten where they're still resting just above my knee. I feel his breath against my neck as he moves closer, his nose tracing my jawline. Our lips are only a hairsbreadth apart, and I can taste his scent on my tongue.

"Whoever hurt you will pay," he whispers, releasing his hold on me and standing up as the doctor enters the room. I'm panting as I watch him move away, and all I want to do is call him back to touch me. The feeling is foreign, but wanted, nonetheless.

"Let's get you patched up," Doctor Barnes mumbles as he starts to clean my wound. It is numb, and I only feel the tugging of the stitches as he works, but my eyes are locked with Jackson's as he stands against the wall.

"We will need to remove these in a few weeks," he says as he finishes.

"Can I shower now?" I ask. On his nod, I thank the good doctor and escape to the bathroom where I lock the door and turn on the water.

I need time away from Jackson Pace.

He makes the feelings I've buried deep inside me resurface, and I don't know how to deal with any of it. The need for him and his power is a deep ache inside me that I have to ignore until I can find Vyper and kill him.

Chapter 15
Jackson

I want to know who hurt her.

I want to kill the son of a bitch that put the fear in her eyes, and I will find him while I hunt for Vyper.

"We have a hit on Vyper," Cyrus says as I enter my office next door to the guest room Morgan is using. The doctor left, promising to come back to check her stitches next week, but I honestly don't think she will be around long enough to see the healing through. "He used his credit card at a hotel about twenty miles north of Baton Rouge."

"Roman?"

"Is on his way now," Cyrus promises with a nod.

I lean back in my chair and wipe my hand

over my face. The stress of everything is wearing me down, and knowing Morgan is in the room next to me is driving me insane with lust.

I almost kissed her. It was a mistake. She is not mine, but fuck if I want her…all of her. With her fear, I don't know what she's been through, but I have an idea. The thought of her being hurt the same way her clients have been sends anger through my veins like I've never felt. My need for vengeance and blood is like the taste of expensive wine on my tongue.

"I want him taken to the club," I order. "Vyper is not to be brought here as long as Morgan is on my property."

"Done," Cyrus states.

"I'm going to check on her and try to get some sleep," I admit, standing up from my seat. "Check in with Lola and have her email tonight's numbers."

"Yes, sir." Cyrus leaves me without another word. The man has worked for me for several years, and I trust him with my life. Lola runs the club when I'm not there. She's been with me just as long. I trust them both with my life.

I knock on the door to Morgan's room and wait until she calls out for me to enter. I freeze when I enter, finding her standing in the doorway of the bathroom wrapped in nothing but a white towel. Her hair is twisted up in another one, and I can't avert my eyes from the sight before me.

"I don't have any clothes," she grumbles, looking down at herself. She doesn't look away from me in shame, and I am relieved that she's not terrified of being alone with me when she's vulnerable. "I can't wear my others. They're covered in blood."

"I have something you can wear." I clear my throat and turn on my heel. It only takes me a few seconds to get to my room down the hallway. I grab a pair of basketball shorts and a black cotton shirt, returning to her room. "These might be a little large on you."

"Thank you," she says, disappearing into the bathroom. When she returns, the clothes I gave her hang off her body in a way that is sexier than the towel she was just wearing. The sight of Morgan in my clothes sends a possessive chill up my spine.

"How's the arm?"

"It's fine," she responds, tucking her feet under her as she climbs up onto the bed. "The doctor left some pain meds for me." She looks at the unmarked bottle on the dresser and frowns. It's obvious she needs them but is fighting it because she doesn't feel safe.

"You should take the medicine and get some

sleep," I urge, moving to sit at the end of the bed. "You are safe, Morgan. No one will hurt you here."

"I trust you...I think," she says, chewing on her bottom lip.

"What have you heard about me?" I figure we should clear the air. Morgan is a part of the underworld in New Orleans. She has to know how deadly I am.

"You are a dangerous man, Jackson." She shrugs, only using the side that doesn't hurt her. "It's not a secret that you deal in things that are not honest. Your men fear you."

"As well they should," I answer, going for honesty. "I have certain...businesses I conduct that require a heavy hand in leadership. The men who work for me are loyal. If one of them doesn't obey my rules, they are disposed of."

"So, Vyper?" she asks.

"Vyper pledged his loyalty to me as one of my enforcers," I begin, watching Morgan carefully. Her face is tight from the pain she's enduring to stay alert. I hope to put her at ease, and maybe coax her into giving up information on her past. The past few days have made me very protective of the huntress, and I need to know everything about her. "He broke my number one rule when he violated that girl he was seeing."

"You know what happened to her?"

"One of my men visited her in the hospital late one night," I admit, shaking my head to clear the sight of the woman.

"The family didn't tell me anyone came to see her."

"They didn't know," I sigh. "My man went in after hours, took photos of the girl for me, and got out before he was seen."

"It's bad," she whispers, closing her eyes. "Brooke is the reason why I do what I do. No one should have to endure that type of abuse, Jackson."

"What about you?" I ask, taking a chance on a hunch. Morgan was obviously hurt at some point in her life. I want to know who it was. "Who hurt you?"

"I can't tell you," she says, fidgeting with the hair tie on her wrist. I've noticed she pops the band against her skin when she's anxious. "It's too dangerous."

"More dangerous than me?"

"Possibly," she shivers.

"I cannot protect you if you don't tell me the truth about who you really are, Morgan," I push.

"I don't need your protection," she argues.

I reach over and cover the hand she's using to

pop the hair tie, stopping her. She looks at my hand, and then back up into my eyes. There is something between us, and I move closer to her. She doesn't stop me as I lean closer. Just like before, I am caught in her web.

"Well, you are going to have it," I state as I press my lips to hers. The crack of her palm against my face separates us as she scrambles from the bed.

"Don't you ever do that again!"

Chapter 16
Morgan

Jackson Pace is the first man to kiss me in a few years. The shock of his advances sends me into a defensive panic. When his swings around, I see the bright red outline of my hand and I cover my mouth with a loud gasp. "Oh my god! I'm so sorry."

"It's okay, Morgan." He blinks, looking at me like I am someone else entirely. I am. I'm not myself when it comes to a man's interest.

"No," I shake my head, "I shouldn't have slapped you."

"I wouldn't have wanted you to let me continue to kiss you if you didn't want it," he says, standing up from his seat. He's upset, and I can see the pain of rejection in his eyes. I reach out for him, but he steps away. "Take your medicine and get some sleep. Roman or Cyrus will be outside of your door tonight if you need anything."

"Jackson! Wait!"

"Go to bed, Morgan," he orders as he reaches the door.

"I…I was brutally raped and left for dead when I was seventeen," I blurt out. "The man who did it was the vice president of my father's MC. Once my father took his side, and I was able to leave the hospital, I changed my name and moved away. I've been on the run ever since, and I've dedicated my life to taking out men just like him."

Jackson doesn't speak, he just turns slowly in my direction. The anger on his face is something I have never seen before, and I stand my ground. I know deep inside he's not angry at me, but at what I just told him.

"I want his name," he demands, his hands fisting at his side. The green in his eyes has darkened to almost black, and I find myself drawn to his power. He doesn't scare me, and I find comfort in the darkness.

"No," I shake my head, "If you go looking for him, he will know where I am. Rumor has it that he wants me dead."

"Not on my watch," Jackson growls.

"Where's your father?"

"I returned a month later and killed him," I answer. I hated the man who sired me, and I have no remorse.

"Your mother?"

"He killed her."

Jackson returns to the side of the bed and takes a seat. I don't move over and his hip touches my thigh. I run my finger under the hair tie at my wrist and just stare into his eyes. The darkness I saw earlier is now gone.

He hesitates when he raises his hand, but on my nod, he cups my face with his left hand. The comfort in the gesture is so foreign to me, I feel something inside my cold heart crack. I don't like it…I do like it. I really don't know what to think. This isn't the first time I've been intimate with a man since my attack. I'm not scared of sex, and I don't have a fear of men. I just want to kill the ones like Vyper and the man who almost killed me all those years ago.

"I will not let him find you," he promises, "but I need his name so that I can find out where he is. It's very important, Morgan."

"I'm not used to having anyone want to protect me, Jackson," I admit, swallowing hard.

"I know you can take care of yourself, but you

have someone out there who wants to kill you, and not because of your underground activities." He pauses, dropping his hand. "I've become very protective of you, and I will stop at nothing to keep you safe."

"As soon as I heal from this wound, I will go after Vyper," I say, changing the subject. "As long as I stay underground, I will be safe."

"I still want a name," he states.

"I'm sorry...I can't tell you," I hedge. "He's too dangerous...more dangerous than you."

"We will see about that," he replies, reaching over for the bottle of pills on the nightstand. "I need you to rest and heal, Morgan. Tomorrow we will talk about this. It's late."

I reluctantly take a pill from the bottle and down it with a bottled water that has gone warm since the doctor left it for me. Jackson is unusually quiet as he pulls back the covers. "I'll stay here until you are asleep. One of my men will be outside of your room tonight, like I promised."

"Okay," I yawn. I'm tired. It's been one hell of a night, and I'm pissed at myself for getting shot, telling him about my past, and slapping him when he tried to kiss me.

Chapter 17
Jackson

"I want the names of MC's whose presidents were murdered approximately seven years ago," I bark into the phone as soon as Cyrus answers the next morning. I didn't sleep much the night before because I was processing the small amount of information she had given me. She won't give me a name, but I have my ways of finding out what I need to know.

"Do you know a state?" he asks.

"No," I reply.

"Morgan?" Cyrus obviously knows I'm talking about the woman staying in the room next to my office. My right-hand man goes silent while he waits for my answer. I can hear the unanswered questions in his silence, but I don't need to tell him how I feel about her. I'm sure I've thrown him because I've never brought a woman to my home. All of my relations have been done at the club. I don't want the nameless faces here.

"Morgan Rayne is not her legal name," I state, remembering what she said. "She's changed it since running away when she was just seventeen. This is all the information I have, for now. I want to know who the VP of that club was and where he is today. I want him brought to me."

"I'll find out what I can," Cyrus answers.

"Do it discretely," I warn, hanging up the phone when I hear the door to her room open. She stalls in the hallway outside of my office. She's still dressed in my clothes, and I notice her hair is back up in the ponytail. Her eyes are clouded from her sleep, and she looks more feminine than usual. Her hardass features have softened, and I want to take her into my arms, but I know she will push me away.

"Good morning," I greet. "Coffee?"

"Please?" She yawns and walks over to take a seat on the couch against the wall to my left. I pick up the phone and call down to the kitchen, asking Moose to bring up some coffee. My housekeeper isn't here today, and I would need to explain the new face to her. Betty doesn't trust new people in my circle. She's just as savage as my men.

"How are you feeling today?"

"Sore," she answers, moving her arm around to test it. "Stiff."

"You will be for a few days."

"I need to go home."

"I will take you home after you've eaten," I promise, standing up to come over to take a seat next to her. "Morgan, we need to talk about last night."

"No, Jackson, we don't," she sighs. "I have stayed hidden for this long. I don't need you interfering with my life because I was wronged."

"I will find him," I vow.

"I'm not yours," she growls. "I don't need you to fight my past for me."

"Are you going to tell me your real name?"

"I'm not that person anymore," she replies. I already knew she wasn't going to tell me that easily. She doesn't trust people, and now I understand why.

"One of these days, you'll tell me," I push, feeling more protective of her than the night before.

"Until then, we need to find Vyper, and quit talking about my past," she urges, changing the subject. I resign myself to letting Cyrus do his work to find out where she came from and who harmed her.

"So, are you saying you will work for me?" I ask.

"As one of your enforcers?" she counters.

"Yes," I nod. "I will hold you to the same standards as I do them."

"I work alone," she reminds me.

"I will double the money Brooke's family is paying you," I offer.

"It's not about the money," she responds. "The families pay me, and I accept it, because it's their way of getting closure, I guess. They seem to use my payment as justification for the things they've asked of me."

"What do you do with the money, then?"

"I donate it to women's shelters and programs in different cities," she says. "Whatever you pay me will go to them anyway."

Moose brings in a tray with coffee and some pastries. I make Morgan a cup of coffee after asking her how she likes it. She moans softly when she takes the first sip and my body responds. I turn away and take my cup back over to my desk to keep my hands off of her.

"I'm sorry I slapped you last night," she blurts, setting her cup down on the table next to the couch.

"I should have had better manners," I say as an apology.

"I live a solitary life, Jackson," she admits, biting her bottom lip. "I don't have a man. I haven't had a man in a long time, and you just took me by surprise."

"By surprise?" I ask, raising a brow. She has to know the affect she has had on me since she was on her knees in my office. "I know you feel something when you are close to me. I can see it in your eyes. Do you not feel it?"

"Your darkness calls to me," she says.

"My soul wants to protect you, even though you can protect yourself," I explain, scooting my chair away from my desk. "I do have a darkness inside me, and when you told me about your past, that darkness wants your attacker's blood. I want to torture him for the things he's done to you."

"That was a long time ago," she says softly as she looks away.

"Still doesn't forgive what he did," I argue, rising to my feet. I walk around my desk and stand in front of her. The softness of her features has fled, and I want to reach out to smooth away the tightness between her eyes, but I refrain. Instead, I take a knee in front of her and hold out my hand. When she takes it into hers, I vow, "I will find the man who hurt you and bring him to you to do with as you will. I promise to let you deal out your own justice, and I won't interfere."

Her hand tightens around mine, and we are frozen as I wait for her reply. I'm shocked, but don't show any emotion when she uses her free hand to cup my face where she'd slapped me the night before. She hesitates as she moves closer, and I hold my breath, waiting. When she leans in, I relax as she presses her lips to mine and releases me just as fast. "Thank you, but I still cannot give you a name."

Chapter 18
Morgan

Saturdays are always busy, and the Quarter is in full swing tonight. The tourists are using their last night in town to party before they go back home to their regular lives. I envy them a little, because this is my regular life. I don't have a nine to five job to dread on Monday mornings. I wouldn't know what to do with myself if I had to sit behind a desk all day.

A hoard of drunken men whistle as I pass, but I don't pay them much attention when I turn off of Bourbon Street to head toward Landry's place. I need to check in with him to see if he's heard any whispers about Vyper.

The store is closed, but I knock on the window to signal I'm outside. It takes him several minutes to come to the front of the store. He looks tired, and I feel bad for bothering him this late, but I need answers.

"Come in," he yawns.

"I need to talk to you," I announce as I push past him. He locks the door and ushers me to the back of the store where he lives in a small apartment.

"Where have you been?"

"Well," I cringe. "About that…"

"Morgan," he drawls, and it sounds like he's scolding me. "I've been looking for you."

"I was interrogated by Jackson Pace, shot, and ended up at his home outside of the city," I tell him.

"Damn it, Morgan." Landry sits down heavily in his chair as he shakes his head in disappointment. "Have you not found Vyper?"

"No," I reply. "That's why I came to talk to you. I need to know what you've heard."

"He's on the run and knows that several people are looking for him. He's been shacking up with someone you know." Landry stands up and walks over to the cabinet over his sink. He removes a piece of paper and hands it over to me. I open it, and immediately drop it to the ground, pushing my chair away from the table.

"How? Why?" I gasp.

"Your past has caught up to your present,"

Landry offers, but I already know it from looking at that black and white photo from a security camera.

"Where was that taken?"

"Baton Rouge," he answers as I fold the paper and tuck it in my boot. "You need to take this guy out...or get the fuck outta da Quarter."

"Duke Hale has no business in this area," I growl, fighting panic and anger. Seeing the man who destroyed me shaking hands on a grainy video with the man I've been hired to kill doesn't make sense. "How in the hell did he find me?"

"I have no idea, Morgan, but you need to let Jackson know...if he doesn't already." Landry nods toward my phone. "Call Mr. Pace."

"No." I shake my head. "I need to end this with Duke and take out Vyper. When did you get this photo?"

"Two days ago."

"I need to go," I say, walking over to kiss Landry on the cheek. He nods and walks me to the door but stops me before I leave.

"You can come here anytime." He shakes my hand, slipping a door key into my palm. I close my hand around it. I pretend to fix my boot, dropping the key down inside for safe keeping. "I'd stay with Jackson Pace if I were you. He's the only man who has the power to keep you alive. Trust him, Morgan."

"Why are you taking Jackson's side now?" I ask as Landry starts closing his door.

"I've always trusted him," he says boldly. "It's the man you're looking for that I don't trust."

"I'll be in touch," I say, escaping into the night.

Landry wants me to trust Jackson. In some ways, I do. In others, I don't. He is after my mark, and I feel it's my duty to take Vyper out. Letting Jackson into my world ensures he will want Vyper for himself. My loyalty is to the girl he left for dead. I must avenge her.

The fact that Jackson Pace heats my body every single time he touches me is a problem. I'm not here for flowers and Saturday night dates. I don't want that at all. I'm not even looking for a man, because most men cannot handle me. The last one I left in the middle of the night because he wanted me to settle down with him. He was delusional if he thought I was going to be the Martha Stewart type.

Checking my surroundings, I start to slide the key into the door to my building but pause. The door is ajar just a fraction of an inch. I lean in closer and feel my heart thunder when I realize the lock has been picked. My home isn't secure anymore, and I need to leave. It pisses me off that I don't have my car keys with me. I don't usually drive out of the Quarter unless necessary, and I'd left them with Roman after being shot.

I walk several blocks away from my apartment and cross the street. There is a coffee shop with patio seating. Trying to figure out who's been snooping around my place, I casually take a seat and order a small coffee to keep my hands busy. From my seat, I don't see any lights on in my place, but that doesn't mean shit if there is someone up there hiding in the dark and waiting to ambush me.

My eyes follow three men as they approach the restaurant under my tiny apartment, but they don't go inside. They hover around the gate that leads to steps up to my door. They don't touch the handle, nor do they look up into the stairwell. I know I'm being paranoid, but there are two men that may be coming for me. I have to be vigilant.

"Morgan?" Jackson answers on the first ring, and I can hear tension in his voice.

"Someone picked the lock to the door at street level to my apartment," I whisper. "I am at the coffee shop a block away having coffee."

"I'm on my way with Roman," he replies.

"Jackson, Vyper knows I'm looking for him,

and he's been hanging out with someone from my past," I admit, keeping my voice low. The sounds of Zydeco music coming from the coffee shop speakers drowns out most of my words, and I cross my leg over my knee so I can have quick access to the gun in my boot. I will not hesitate to kill them, even if I'm sitting at a coffee shop surrounded by innocents.

"Don't you fucking go anywhere, Morgan."

"Not moving from this spot," I promise, hanging up the phone.

Chapter 19
Jackson

When I approach the coffee shop, Morgan tosses a few dollars on the table and stands to greet me. The waitress in the coffee shop nods in my direction as she waits on a customer. She is the wife of one of the bouncers at my club, and from the set to her jaw, I know she's been watching over Morgan.

"Let's go," I mumble as I take her hand. She folds her fingers over mine and begins to walk alongside me. We turn left out of the coffee shop and take a side road to where Roman is parked with my SUV. As soon as we slide into the backseat, he locks us inside.

"What happened?" I ask. Roman pulls away from the curb and heads out of the Quarter. I want her at my home where she will be safe.

"Someone is in my fucking apartment," she growls, clenching her fists.

"Did you see anyone?"

"No." She shakes her head. "The gate leading to the stairwell to my building was ajar, and before you ask, I know it was closed and locked up tight before I left."

"I believe you," I reply. One thing I'd noticed about Morgan Rayne was her severe OCD and nervous tics when it came to every aspect of her life. She wouldn't be as careless as to leave the gate unlocked.

"Thank you," she sighs, leaning back in her seat.

"I will have your apartment checked by my men tonight," I say, shooting off a text to Cyrus. He's going to pull Rocco and Moose from the club and send them over immediately.

"Are you only sending over those two men?" she asks, popping the hair tie at her wrist. She's nervous, and I'm confused. She's not acting like herself. She said that Vyper was working with someone from her past, and I knew exactly who she was referring to when she called me earlier.

"I would never send someone into your apartment that you don't know. You can trust me,

Morgan," I reply, feeling bad about capturing her, but I needed to know the information she had on my man. A hit has been put out on him by the girl's family, but he is my problem to deal with when he's found.

"Thank you," she says, then frowns. "I just have to make sure all of my bases are covered when it comes to my safety and what I do for these women."

"Don't be scared," I say, reaching out to touch her leg. She doesn't look my way, and I wonder if she even heard me. It takes several seconds before she answers.

"I'm not scared," she sighs, "I'm planning how I'm going to kill them."

"We need to talk about this with Cyrus," I order.

"I know." Morgan doesn't look at me as she answers. Her head is turned toward the window as she watches the scenery pass by on our drive. I hear her yawn, but do not comment on it. She needs more rest than she's gotten since meeting me.

"After we have a meeting with Cyrus, you should go to your room and rest," I advise, checking my phone when it pings. My men have reached her apartment and are checking things out. We should have an answer shortly.

"My room?" she laughs and finally turns in

her seat to look at me.

"It's yours to use when you need it."

"As soon as your men clear my apartment, I will get a cab and head back there," she says, narrowing her eyes.

"You can go home tomorrow…if your place is safe," I assert.

"We'll see," she replies, and resumes looking out the window until we arrive at my place.

Roman opens the door for Morgan to exit, and I follow her to the front door where Cyrus is already waiting. I take her hand, ignoring her frown. She could've been attacked by Vyper this evening, and since she's still healing from the gunshot, the huntress could've been overpowered by my man.

That thought alone makes me want to skin him alive.

"Let's go to my office," I suggest, still holding her hand. Cyrus walks behind us silently, and I appreciate his calmness in this situation.

I refuse to let her secrecy go any further. My mind is churning over a million possible outcomes to this situation, and I'm starting to visualize this man from her past as a monster even I cannot destroy. Her silence is beginning to terrify me, and the feeling is feeding my darkness.

Morgan comes to a halt at the threshold of my office, her fingers slowly releasing mine. I turn to look at her, needing to know what it is that has frightened her, and I'm perplexed when I see her staring at Cyrus.

"Morgan?"

"Can we talk about this alone?" she asks, inclining her head toward him.

"Thank you, Cyrus." I dismiss him. "I will call you shortly."

Cyrus nods and backs away, heading toward the kitchen. I walk into the room, but I don't sit in my chair. I lean against the desk instead. Morgan returns to the corner of the couch she'd sat in the first time she was here.

"Would you like a drink?" I offer, hoping it will help her with loosening up a little. I have a feeling what she's about to tell me will need a bit of liquid courage.

"Tequila…a double," she answers. I walk over to the bar and pour her a shot, returning to hand it over. She shoots the liquor and hands me the glass. "You may want to sit down for this."

Turning the chair that sits in front of my desk for my guests, I drag it over as close as I can to the couch, taking a seat. Morgan is still sitting in the same spot, her feet tucked up under her and her damaged arm laying loosely across her stomach.

"Go ahead," I urge.

"Duke," she pauses to clear her throat, "Duke Hale took over as the president of the Painted Devils MC out of Portland after my father died. Somehow, he's made his way to Baton Rouge and is now hanging with Vyper."

"How do you know this?" I growl.

"My contacts have proof," she says, not going into detail about who this contact is or where they are in the city. "Here."

Morgan reaches into her boot and removes a piece of paper, handing it over to me. I carefully unfold the paper to reveal a still photo from a camera mounted outside of a seedy looking bar. It's also a bar that I know very well in the area.

"So, this is the man who harmed you?" I feel the black abyss of my soul churning inside at the hatred I have for this man I don't even know. He's easily the same size as Vyper, and just as heavily tattooed. I can see his face fairly clearly, and the teardrop tattoo on his eye is the first identifier I notice. The other is an anchor tattoo on the right side of his neck.

"Yeah," she moves her feet to plant them on

the floor, "I need a plan to take them both out."

"You're in no shape to go after one, let alone two, men," I remind her.

"Jax, I have never needed help, and I don't need it now." She stands from her seat and folds her arms across her chest. I see her jaw tic as she clenches her teeth. She's angry, but I don't care.

"I'm right, and you know it," I bark, feeling my anger rise at her stubbornness. I stand and square my shoulders. I take two strides and wrap my arm around her waist, pulling her body flush with my own. Her eyes darken, and I breathe deep, reminding myself not to push her too far, but she has to know the effect she has on me.

"You, my little huntress, are stirring feelings inside me that are foreign, and I can't decide if I like it or not," I begin, growling low in my throat when she begins to speak. She presses her lips together to let me finish. "You may fight me on this…you may even shoot me, but you are mine, and I take care of things that harm what belongs to me."

"You cannot claim me," Morgan whispers, her eyes darkening as they trace my lips.

"I can," I say, taking a chance by pressing my lips to hers.

Morgan surprises me by sinking her fingers

into the hair at the nape of my neck and pulling my face closer to hers as her tongue demands entrance. I feel my cock harden beneath my fly as she nips at my bottom lip.

"I should slap you again," she hums.

"Then stop kissing me," I tease.

"Shut up, Jackson," she orders, and takes my lips again.

My hands skim down her side to cup her ass. She doesn't push me away. I'm careful of her arm as I hold her tight against me. She is warm and womanly despite her hardass nature. The feel of her lips against mine sends my heart into a spiral. Morgan is tender yet demanding.

"We should stop," I mumble against her lips. It's one of the hardest things I've ever done, but I pull away and release my hold on her.

"I don't want to stop," she pleads, "but I must tell you something before we continue."

"What is that?" I ask.

"There's something I must show you." She breathes deeply. Her hands grasp the bottom of her shirt and I tilt my head to the side in confusion. "I want you to see me like this before we become intimate."

"You're worrying me," I admit as I move to

take a step toward her. She stands her ground and narrows her eyes. She doesn't want me close.

"He did things to me," she whispers, and lifts her shirt. My eyes blink several times as the skin on her belly becomes visible. She's toned and muscular from working out, but what shatters my heart are the seven scars across her stomach. They start just under her ribcage and disappear into her jeans below her belly button. There is no pattern to them…just scars from being cut.

"Duke did this?" I ask, trying to control my temper.

"He carved me," she says, her voice strong. I expect her to break, but she doesn't. Morgan is stronger than I thought. "The ones lower are deeper. He actually stabbed me, and the damage was irreparable."

"Irreparable?" I frown, a host of doctors run through my mind that I can have attend to her. Whatever Duke did, we can fix this.

"I had a hysterectomy because of the stab wounds," she offers.

"I am truly sorry," I say, walking up to her. I lift my hand and cup her cheek. "You are beautiful."

Morgan smiles and leans in for a kiss. She isn't shy, nor does she take her time. I take a step back and stop when the back of my legs hit the chair I'd been sitting in a moment before. Morgan pushes my shoulder and my ass hits the chair. She grins wickedly and swings her long leg over my lap. I feel the warmth of her pussy through her denim jeans when she settles in over my hard cock. I close my eyes and lean my head back as she kisses me again. She is a seductress, and I am caught in her web.

"This doesn't change who I am," she admits.

"You are not ready for a man like me," I warn, but it dies on my tongue.

"I'm no virgin, Jackson," she states, leaning away from me, but only slightly. I see the light sheen of sweat on her neck, and I press my hand between her shoulders to bring her to my tongue. I lick the column of her neck and fist my hand in the back of her hair. I will forever crave the taste of the sweet and saltiness of her skin.

"My needs are more than you can handle," I offer, warning her away from me.

"My needs are not conventional either," she replies, taking my hand to guide it to her breast. "I ache."

Chapter 20
Morgan

I'm on fire from the need for him. Despite every warning bell going off in my mind, my body doesn't care…it wants this man.

I look down to see the back of his tattooed hand as it's cupping my breast. The back of his hand is tattooed with a skull, but only the eyes, nose, and upper teeth are there with blue shading the background. The word LOVE is spelled out across his four fingers. The need to tear my shirt off and have him press his skin to mine is overwhelming. I want to ask him to touch my other breast, but at the moment, I cannot form words to tell him exactly what I need.

"You like watching me touch you, don't you?" he asks as he finds my hardened nipple beneath the material of my shirt and my lace bra. He rolls it between his fingers, and I throw my head back at the bite of pleasured pain. The sensation shoots straight to my core, and I feel wetness pool between my legs.

"Yes," I reply.

"What else do you like?" he taunts, gripping my hips.

I take a deep breath, because I need the extra time to form my words. Jackson Pace could be my downfall. He could easily destroy me if I open up a part of who I used to be, but I trust him…I trust his darkness.

"This," I hum.

"What else, Morgan?" he demands in that dark, sultry voice. My muscles hum beneath the skin that covers them, the need for release builds and flexes between my legs. The wetness there is a sure sign that I want him.

"I like to *feel*," I whisper, telling him exactly what I need. "I want to let go of it all, and I need a man I can trust and who is willing to take over control from me so I don't have to be on guard when he's between my legs."

"You need a man you can trust," he breathes, nipping at my chin. His fingertips flutter across the exposed skin above my waistband. The contact is hot, electric, and I want more. "I can protect you when you need to let down your guard."

"Promise?" I breathe. My voice is soft, and I don't recognize my own sound.

"Promise," he nods, pulling my lips to his own. The metal on his lip piercing is hot against my bottom lip, and I nibble at the ring as I roll my hips to rub myself against him.

"Jackson!" I gasp when he stands, holding me tight against his body as he leaves his office. I'm worried that someone will see us, but there is no one around when he walks across the foyer and into his bedroom on the other side of his home.

My eyes take in the luxurious bedroom when he sets me on the king size bed against the far wall. The walls are dark gray, and the bedding is a shade lighter. There is an old fireplace to my left. Ahead of me is the door we entered through, and on my right is a door to what I assume is a bathroom. There is only one painting and it hangs above the fireplace. The art is something from one of the locals in the area. I've seen his work before in a gallery in the Quarter.

"Tell me now if you don't want this," Jackson says as he removes his shirt. I trace the artwork on his chest. The wings of an owl spread across his chest, the tips touching his shoulders. My fingers itch to trace the ink on his skin.

"I do," I admit, still breathless. I may be in an unknown place, but I feel at home. It should scare the fuck out of me, but it doesn't.

With a flick of his thumb and forefinger, he releases the top button of his jeans and presses one knee into the bed, leaning over me. I melt further into the pillow beneath my head when he kisses me again.

I hear his boots hit the ground; one, then the other. His hand is on my face as his tongue explores my mouth and he's using his other arm to hold his weight off of me. The air is heating around us, and I hook my fingers in his waistband, giving his jeans a tug. He releases my face and gently pulls my hand away from his jeans. "Patience, Ms. Rayne."

A strange feeling tugs at the center of my chest, and I ignore it. The craving to bury myself under his skin causes me to shiver, and I hide it by reaching behind me to unhook my bra. Jackson loops a finger under each strap and slowly draws them down my arms. His lips touch my shoulder, my bicep. I shiver from the softness of this dangerous man.

"I must taste you," he groans, making one long pass over my sensitive nipple. My legs begin to saw against his hips as he gives the other one just a much attention.

This deadly man, with hands capable of

destruction, touches my body with a tenderness I never expected. I lift my head when he removes the hair tie I have in my hair. Before I can comment, Jackson sits back on his knees and slowly rolls the band onto my wrist. He knows its worth to me and doesn't take it from my reach. I feel that heaviness in my chest again.

My fingers tangle in his hair and pull him back to my lips. I cannot get enough of his lips. The warmth reminds me of a favorite blanket on a cold winter night. I relax into his touch just a little more. The ferocity of my need for him settles deep between my legs. "Touch me…undress me, Jackson."

He frees my button and zipper, tucking his hand between my skin and the material. I feel the trail of heat as he slides his hand around to my side so he can remove my jeans. I don't complain when he takes my black lace panties with them. Cool air hits my toes when my boots are tossed to the ground. I gasp and sit up, reaching for my weapon that stays strapped to my ankle. Jackson leans back and allows me to disarm, moving my gun to the side table to my left. I am so deep in the pleasure, I forgot to take the gun out of the holster in my boot. It says a lot for me to rest my gun on my non-dominate side. The unspoken action doesn't go unnoticed. Jackson nods as if he understands I'm trusting him.

"Nice concealed piece." He smiles appreciatively. Only a man like Jackson Pace would praise me for the gun I keep hidden for my protection while he was well on his way to being buried between my legs.

"Touch me or I'll use it on you," I plead. Jackson chuckles and cups my breast only a second before he takes the other one between his teeth. There is pleasured pain in his touch, and I respond appropriately. I automatically raise my hips in a silent plea for more.

"Easy," he warns, pushing my hips back to the bed. He reaches over into his side table drawer and removes a foil pack. He tears it with his teeth and his hand disappears between us.

I'm thankful the lights are off and only a dim light is coming from his attached bathroom. I'm not ashamed of my body, but the scars I keep hidden tell a story of my past with Duke. I've learned to ignore them and to not let them define who I am.

My body jolts when his fingers graze my pussy. He only uses his thumb to test my wetness. A deep, masculine sound comes from his chest as he takes my lips again. I wrap my arms around his neck and hold him tight when he pushes his finger inside me. "Wrap your legs around me, baby."

I do as I'm told, and the new position allows him to slide deeper inside me to the spot that craves his attention. I protest when he removes his hand but breathe a sigh of relief when he guides himself into my body. My nails sink into his shoulder blade as he seats himself fully. The erotic glide of his cock threatens to set me off into an orgasm of epic proportions, but I fight it. I want to make this last for the both of us.

"I'm going to make you come around my cock," he smirks as he pulls back from my lips. "After that, I want to taste you when you scream my name." Oh, my. I'm going to die from this. I just know it.

He lifts my hips and thrusts once, twice, and the inside of my thighs begin to quiver. I can't hold out for long. He's commanding my body with each movement. My pussy clamps down on his cock and I feel the stirrings of my release.

"So close," I choke out. The sounds coming from me are erotic and thick with desire. Again, Jackson Pace is working his way into the hardened shell around my heart. I feel another crack when he cups my face with the hand he was using on my hip. The tenderness is foreign, but somehow wanted.

"Give it to me," he demands, increasing his strokes.

"No," I tease, holding off my release. I want more of the buildup. I need more of his closeness.

"My little huntress," he whispers, and shakes his head as he smirks. He's accepted the challenge, and I am ready for the game.

I slide my leg down the outside of his and press the flat of my foot to the bed. In one quick move, I roll him over onto his back, not once dislodging his cock from deep inside me. Jackson's eyes darken as I sit astride him, and his hands grasp the tops of my thighs. He raises his hips to remind me that he is in control, and I lean over to grab the headboard to keep from falling against his chest. The position puts my breasts right at mouth level and he uses that advantage to take one of my nipples into his mouth, biting down hard enough to make the pain shoot straight to my core.

The moment he takes the other nipple, I am a slave to my release. The heat coils around me, and I am frozen as I whimper into the darkened room. He senses my need and rolls us, dominating me so he can give what I am needing. My voice is deep, and my eyes are fixated on his as he drives into me. "More…harder."

"Fuck," he curses as I feel his cock pulse inside me, but his seed is caught by the condom. He thrusts several more times as we both crash from our release.

Jackson falls to my right and pulls me against his side. We are both breathing deeply and covered in sweat. I need a shower, but I have no care in the world to even move.

I am content.

Chapter 21
Morgan

I slip out of Jackson's bed an hour after he's fallen asleep. When I open the door to his room, I see Roman walking up the hallway. He's not wearing the usual suit, and I'm taken aback seeing him in workout clothes.

"Please tell me Jax has a home gym," I tease, meeting the guard in the hallway.

"Yes, Jackson does." A small smirk plays at the corner of his mouth as he shakes his head. "Has he told you that he hates that nickname?"

"Nope," I smirk. "I'll have to remember that."

"So, were you looking to workout, or were you going to escape into the night?" Roman relaxes and leans against the wall.

"Actually," I shrug, "I'm hungry. Is there any

food in this place?"

"Yes," he says, then turns. "I'll show you to the kitchen."

Beyond the hallway that leads back to the foyer, and the only place I've seen in his home besides his office and the bedroom I used the first time I was here, there is a huge living area and an equally massive kitchen. I freeze when we enter and see an older female standing over a sink.

"Betty," Roman says when the woman turns and rakes me with her eyes. She is suspicious of me, and I really don't blame her. I'm a new face in this hidden kingdom of illegal activity. Jackson Pace only hires those who are loyal to him. "This is Morgan, and she is one of us."

"Mr. Jackson knows she's here?" Betty confirms with a slight Cajun drawl.

"Yes," Roman chuckles. "She is his guest and should be treated as such."

"Good…good," she says, slinging water off of her hands. "May I get you something, Ms. Morgan?"

"It's late," I say, shaking my head. "If you have some fruit, I can take care of myself."

"Ah, yes," Betty smiles. "I have some freshly cut." Betty removes a divided container from the fridge and sets it on the island bar in the middle of the kitchen. She dismisses herself and leaves the room.

"Don't mind Betty," Roman says, taking a seat next to me and opening the container. He pops a strawberry in his mouth and smiles. "She's like a mama bear to us."

"I see." I nod and grab a piece of pineapple. "She doesn't like me."

"She doesn't like anyone." Roman grabs a grape and another strawberry before walking around the island to the large stainless steel fridge. "Wine?"

"Please," I respond.

Roman pulls two glasses from the cabinet. He pours and hands one over to me. I take a sip and set it next to the fruit. He returns to his seat and grabs another grape. "Vyper is in the area."

"I know," I reply, reaching for another pineapple piece. I don't want to think about what he's doing with Duke, but I need to stay vigilant. The time is now to plan but having Jackson and his men around will make it hard. I'm afraid they will get in my way.

"You need to let us help you." Roman takes a drink from his glass and sets it down, rolling the stem of the glass between his palms. I'm fascinated how delicate he is with the expensive glass despite his large hands. He holds it as if it's precious. "I don't think you know just how fucked up he is."

"I have a very good idea of what I'm dealing with, Roman," I say, making a fist on the granite bar top. "It's very important that I take this man out on my own."

"Why?"

"It's safer for everyone." I shrug. "Plus, I've been hired to do it."

"But he belongs to Jackson." Roman mimics my shrug and downs the rest of his wine, taking his glass to the sink. I follow his lead and rinse mine before turning it upside down.

"What do you mean by that?"

"When we pledge ourselves to Jackson, it's for life," he replies, returning to the stool and swiveling to face me. "There are a lot of things we do for him in this city, and Jackson takes care of us as long as we stay loyal."

"What if you want to leave?" I inquire. I need to know everything about what I'm getting into with Jackson Pace.

"We retire," he says, not elaborating on what that entails. It makes me think the worst and knowing what I do about the underground of this city, Jackson Pace could make anyone he knows disappear if he wanted them gone. "Do you want to go workout that arm?"

Roman changes the subject, and I'm thankful. He is the only one I somewhat trust besides Jackson, and even my trust in him is sketchy.

"Sure." I slip off the stool and follow him out the back door. Across the backyard, we enter a pool house full of workout equipment and a large area covered in mats for sparring.

The clock over the door says it's only fifteen minutes past midnight, and I should be tired but I'm not. Walking over to the weights, I choose something light to begin. The first curl is painful on my left arm, but it's bearable. After about thirty reps, I change hands. I'm going slowly while Roman is on the treadmill. He's put on headphones and isn't even looking my way.

A warm breeze caresses my skin as I return the weight to the rack. When I look over my shoulder, Jackson is standing there with sleepy eyes. He looks toward Roman, who hits the button on the machine and steps off, giving me a nod before leaving the building.

"I thought maybe you'd left," Jackson says as he leans against the door. He's wearing a pair of jogging pants and a soft, blue cotton shirt. He looks comfortable and less like the dangerous man I know.

"No," I say with a shake of my head. "I'm

going to listen to you and make sure my apartment is clear before heading home."

"It's clear," he says, pushing off the door. "Rocco said someone had been in there because the lock to your door was broken. Nothing inside had been disturbed."

"Good." I breathe a sigh of relief.

"He also said you have nothing inside of value," Jackson continues, narrowing his eyes. "Why in the hell do you live in that place?"

"I don't need anything else," I admit, looking around the pool house as if to remind myself. "I don't need luxury, Jax."

"You deserve to live in a home that isn't in the worst part of the Quarter," he says, pushing away from the wall. "You deserve more than what you allow yourself."

"I've never lived with much," I sigh, remembering my past life. "Even as a kid, I had the bare minimum. My parents didn't have much, and what money we did have, my father used it to build the club."

"What about after you left?" he pushes. I trust him more now, and I know whatever he is asking is for his own curiosity and not to harm or use against me.

"I went to Seattle for about three months. I lived on the streets and begged for money." I look up at him. "When I had enough to move on, I made it as far as Denver. I really liked it there, and I found a job as a waitress."

"What made you decide to come here? To do the things you do?" he asks, taking my hand with his. The gesture is more than comforting, and even with his darkness, there's a passion about Jackson Pace that calls to my feminine side.

"In Denver, I worked for the sweetest lady." I pause, trying to not cry. "Kristen was the owner of the diner where I worked. She paid me under the table and gave me a room above the place for free. One night a few hours after we'd closed, I heard a commotion coming from the kitchen. When I went to investigate, I found her husband beating her. He was trying to rape her, and I lost it."

"What did you do, Morgan?"

"I took a knife from the butcher block and stabbed him in the neck," I admitted. "He fell to the floor and was dead within a few minutes."

"What did the police do?"

"I don't know," I answer, wiping away a stray tear. "Kristen went to the safe and pulled out an envelope. She shoved it in my hands and told me to go. She promised me she would make up a story and cover for me. I ran upstairs and packed my bag. I didn't have much even then, so it only took me a few minutes. I left out the back door and I hopped in my car. I drove the rest of the night and into the next day. Before I knew it, I was here."

"What happened to Kristen?" Jackson's face was solid as stone. I couldn't get a read on what he was thinking, and that worried me.

"I never contacted her after I left."

"I can look for her…if you'd like," he offers. His thumb strokes the back of my hand to give comfort and I place my hand over his to stop him.

"I don't think that would be a good idea."

"How did you get involved with the underground in New Orleans?"

"I beat up a guy who had pinned a woman in a darkened shop entrance around two in the morning, and a man got me out of there before the cops could arrive." I pause, not sure how much I want to tell him about Landry. "He let me stay with him for a few months, and I kept saving these women who were being mugged, groped, and two of them were beaten almost to the point of death."

"So, this *friend*," Jackson begins, narrowing his eyes. "What did he say about your activities?"

"He agreed with me." I shrug. "He paid for me to take Krav Mara classes, and once I mastered that, I went on to other classes. I could fight MMA, but I chose to stay underground when I had a woman offer me money to teach her ex-husband a lesson. I guess, after that, I was pegged as "The Huntress" and the calls for help started coming in."

"Have you ever thought about why you do this?" he continues with his questions. I have a feeling he is trying to get inside my head.

"No, it's just what I do." I frown. What is he trying to say?

"You're playing with your life, Morgan," he scolds. "Putting yourself in front of these monsters is like playing roulette."

"This isn't about me," I remind him. "This is about them…the ones who cannot protect themselves."

"No." He shakes his head. "This…what you do…it is about you and some sense of getting revenge for what was done to you."

"I will get my revenge on Duke," I snarl, "but don't you ever think that my helping these families is because of my past. Someone needs to get rid of these scum, Jackson. God knows our laws are not harsh enough on them."

"I agree with you, but let's worry about what we know and spend tomorrow finding out the things we don't. Come to bed?"

I take his hand and reluctantly follow him back to his room. I climb in the bed after removing my jeans and bra. I figure I can come up with a plan during the next few hours while I wait for sleep to come, but I feel my body relaxing as Jackson rolls over and pulls my back to his chest. It only takes me another minute or two before I fall fast asleep.

Chapter 22
Morgan

The morning comes, and I snuggle back down into the bed. My body refuses to move, but I know I need to get up and check my phone for any missed messages. Jackson forced me to turn it off before bed, and I did so reluctantly.

When I power it up, I see that I didn't miss any calls, but the most disturbing thing is the time is right at noon. I slept for about ten hours. I don't ever remember a time when I laid my head down and slept so soundly. A little voice in the back of my head tells me that it's because I'm with Jackson, and my subconscious trusts him to keep me protected.

I ignore that voice and make my way to the shower. It doesn't take me long to put on my clothes and pull my towel-dried hair up into a sloppy bun. I have no desire to do anything else. I'm hungry, and I don't know where Jackson is.

Roman and Jackson are sitting at the kitchen table when I enter. Both men are reading the paper as I locate a fresh pot of coffee waiting for me. I find a cup in the cabinet and make myself at home. When I turn around, Jackson is staring at me over the top of his paper, and Roman is nowhere to be found. He must've slipped out as soon as I poured my coffee. I didn't even hear him move.

"Good morning," I yawn, and take a seat.

"Afternoon, Morgan," he chuckles, and closes his paper, setting it on the table in front of him.

"Yeah, I slept a long time." I frown.

"You don't sleep much?" he asks.

"Only a few hours a night," I admit, and take a sip of coffee.

"I want you to turn off your phone and live a little tonight," he says, resting his folded hands on top of the table. I see the fire in his eyes I crave and a small smile tugs at the corners of my lips.

"Live a little?" I chuckle. "It's been a long time since I've had any fun."

"We will go to the club tonight," he says, standing up to take his cup to the sink. "I want you to enjoy yourself."

"That actually sounds nice," I agree.

I finally talk Jackson into letting Keon take me to one of my favorite boutiques in the Quarter to shop for something to wear for the night. Honestly, I don't have much in the way of club clothes.

We arrive back at Club Phoenix just as the sun is setting. When I enter the apartment, Jackson is waiting on me, and I accept the shot of tequila he pours before he makes his own.

"Get dressed and we will head down together," he says in a sultry tone that makes my body respond.

I hurry into the guest bathroom and pull on a pair of stretchy black shorts over black hose and a white tank top. Because I feel more comfortable in my tall, black boots, I put them on and slip my gun down inside for easy access. I may be planning on letting my hair down tonight, but I refuse to be unprotected.

Jackson's eyes heat when I enter the living area of his apartment. He clears his throat and approaches me. His thumb and forefinger capture my chin and he guides my lips to his. "I want you to enjoy yourself tonight."

"Oh, I plan on it," I say with a wink and take a step back.

* * *

"Tequila, double," I say as I take a seat. The woman that served me the first time is behind the bar and slides over my drink.

"It's on the house," she says.

"No, it's not," I argue, sliding over a twenty. "If Jackson won't take my money, then put that in your tip jar."

"I think I'm going to like you," she chuckles and drops the money in her bra. She holds out her hand and smiles. "My name is Lola."

"Morgan." I nod and take her hand.

Jackson is holding court with his men, and I have no desire, or need, to be over at the VIP table. I want to watch the club for any sign of Vyper, regardless of me taking the night off. I don't know if he will show up here, but I like to hope that he will. He obviously knows he's in trouble, and my wishes are probably all for naught.

The night before, in Jackson's bed, was some of the best sleep I'd had in seven years. I woke up late and refreshed. Jackson had pampered me all day until it was time to have lunch. A meal was brought to us, and he kissed me with a needy passion I'd never experienced before.

"He watches your every move." Lola smiles as she wipes down the counter. I toss back my shot and look over at where he is sitting. His eyes are on me even though his lips are moving as he speaks to his men.

"He does," I admit, turning around to face her. My back is to Jackson, but that doesn't mean I don't feel his power. No matter where I am in the room, whenever he enters, I feel his gaze like a possessive touch, and I'll admit I'm becoming addicted to it.

A few young men sidle up to the bar and ask for beers. Lola sets a bottle down hard in front of the guy next to me when he stares a little too long. "These seats are taken. Get your beer and move out to the floor." She smiles widely and tacks on a "Thank you" for good measure.

"You didn't need to do that," I scold, waving my hand over my shot glass. She returns with the tequila and pours another shot. When I reach out to drop another twenty in her jar, she grabs my hand.

"No, Morgan. Once was enough."

"Too bad," I tease, giving her a slight wink.

"Tell you what," she says, then pauses, tucking the bar towel into her back pocket. "Dance with me on my break and I won't bother you about the tips."

"When is your break?" I laugh a little when she raises her hand to a passing waitress. She hops up on the bar and swings her legs over to rest on the stool next to me.

"Right now," she grins. "Here, take your shot and let's go."

Lola holds the glass to my lips and I give her a little smirk. She pushes the shot back as I open my mouth, letting it slide down my throat. She sets the glass behind her and hops down, taking my hand in hers.

The music is loud and there is already a crowd gathering on the dance floor. The raised platform for the two performers is empty, but when the girl with the microphone sees us, she calls out for Lola.

"Our lovely barmaid, Lola, has a hot little plaything tonight." The woman smiles, looking out over the crowd. "I think you two need to come up here and show these people how it's done!"

The crowd roars, and the men holler loudly over the deep bass of the song that's playing. I don't even blush when Lola gives my hand a tug. I may never do anything for myself, but I was on the dance team in my high school and I haven't forgotten how to do it.

I glance at the VIP section of the club and see Jackson pause in whatever it is that he's saying to his men. I give him a wink a split second before Lola spins me around to face her. She throws her hands in the air and I follow her lead.

The music vibrates my chest. I close my eyes when the lights start to swirl around our bodies. I feel Lola's knee slide between my legs, and when I open my eyes, she's close. I begin to sway my hips, placing a hand on her shoulder. Her long braids brush over my fingers as she dances. I don't pull away when she rests her hand on my hip, her fingers contacting with the exposed skin where my shirt has ridden up on the side.

"You're good," she flirts and grinds against me as the crowd swells from watching two women dancing seductively.

"You're not so bad yourself." I smile and extend my arms over the tops of her shoulders. Our pelvises are grinding against each other and I turn to look over my shoulder at Jackson. His eyes are on us, and I see the heat in his gaze. He likes what he sees.

The chick with the microphone calls up a few more ladies, and we finish out the song with them. Lola high-fives me, and we head back over to the bar. She slides over another double shot of Tequila and waves off my money, yet again.

"Jackson wants to see you," Roman grunts as he approaches. Lola nods, and after a promise to come back later, I follow the big bodyguard over to the VIP section. The moment I see him, my body responds, and I want nothing more than to take him back upstairs to work off all of the energy I built up while on the stage.

"Lola likes you," he states as I slide in the booth.

"I like her," I shrug. "How was your little meeting, and am I going to like what you have to tell me?" I'm not oblivious. I know they were discussing me, Vyper, and Duke. The fact that I let my hair down for thirty minutes doesn't lessen my resolve to give up on the two men.

"I think it's too dangerous for you to be out on your own," he states, and take a sip of his bourbon. My good mood falters.

"That's funny." I shake my head and pause to gather my words. "I don't need your permission. I will continue to hunt them both."

"Vyper likes to torture his women," Jackson finally says after taking two more gulps of his drink. "I didn't know this until after he'd come to work for me."

"He's a sadist?"

"He's the devil, Morgan," Jackson admits. "I will kill a man for disrespecting me. I will torture and maim a man who ever lays a hand on you, because I assure you Vyper finds sick satisfaction in his work. He will use those tactics if he overpowers you when you find him."

"Sounds like he and Duke are made for each other." I roll my eyes and sit back in my seat when the waitress arrives with another round of drinks. The waitress eyes me, her long, blonde ponytail slapping her shoulder when she turns on her heel and quickly leaves the VIP section. I don't put much weight into her attitude, because I trust Jackson has a strict hold on his employees, and if anyone was out of line, they wouldn't be working for him very long. "You don't have to worry about me, Jackson. I know what I'm doing."

"You are not going after them alone, and that is final," he orders, and I raise a brow. Does he really think I will listen to him?

"I'm leaving," I announce, and turn to leave, but a heavy hand latches onto my elbow.

"You're staying here tonight," he growls, pulling me against his chest when he stands. I feel his hot breath on my neck, and I control a shiver as his authority rolls up my spine. I don't, however, silence the groan of longing that rolls off my tongue. "Food has arrived upstairs. I will feed you and we will go to bed."

I don't even have time to come up with a rebuke before Roman and Cyrus make a barrier around us and we are walking. Lola gives me a saucy wink as we pass the bar, but she doesn't come to my aide. I guess I'm stuck here until things get quiet tonight. Then I will leave and start my hunt without anyone to tell me otherwise.

There is an amazing smell when we enter the apartment. My stomach growls loudly and Jackson takes my hand, silently pulling me toward the kitchen. Two covered platters greet us at the small formal table. He pulls a chair out, and I sit down, placing my hands in my lap.

"This smells so good," I groan, closing my eyes in bliss when he removes the silver domes over the plates. I already know it's steak before I open my eyes.

"Eat," he orders, and takes his seat.

I pick up the knife and cut into the meat, lifting the piece to my lips. When the food touches my tongue, I glance at Jackson through my lowered lashes. He's watching me with his own brand of evil in his eyes.

The darkness is back, and like an invisible thread, it binds us. We are more alike than I want to admit. We are both killers. We are both alphas. The thought of that makes my body heat with desire. I have to control my feelings around him, but my body defies my wishes and I shift in my seat to relieve the tension between my legs.

He copies my move as he eats, and it becomes a game of erotic flirting. Actions speak volumes as we continue to eat, but never break our gazes. No one is around. The apartment is nothing more than a ghost town and we are its sole inhabitants.

The fork drops from my fingertips and clatters on the plate when I hear a low growl come from him. Jackson is already on his feet when I begin to stand. His lips crash down on mine, and anything I want to say to him dies on my tongue.

My hand tangles in the hair at the base of his neck, and I groan when he envelopes me with his arms. I should push him away, but it's impossible. The feel of his hard, powerful body against mine sends need to my bones.

"Need you now," Jackson groans around my lips as I pull back and nip at his lip piercing.

"What are you waiting for?" I taunt.

Jackson scoops me up into his arms and begins walking toward his room. He stops as soon as we cross the threshold and kicks the door closed. I wiggle to silently tell him to release me. For a second, I don't think he wants to lose our connection. I capture his lips in a silent promise that I'm not denying him.

Our bodies collide in a tangle of arms and legs as we fall to the bed. Our clothes are nothing more than piles on the ground. He doesn't speak as he rolls me over and lifts my hips into the air. I groan with lust when he seats himself deep inside me. My hand reaches back to hold onto his upper thigh as he begins to thrust.

His lips meet the back of my neck when he leans over, capturing me and rutting inside me with heavy, punishing thrusts. It's animalistic…it's a claiming, and I relish in his power. "Oh, God."

Chapter 23
Jackson

She's already gone when I wake the next morning. I curse and grab my phone, asking Cyrus if he saw her leave. When he replies that no one had seen her since the night before, I jump to my feet. "I'll be ready to go in twenty minutes. Have the car ready so we can go to her place. With Vyper in the area, I don't want her alone."

I hurry through my shower and shave, tossing on a button-down dress shirt with my black jeans. This afternoon, I have a meeting with the liquor distributor, and after that, I'm needed at the warehouse in Hammond.

"Boss," Cyrus calls as I round the corner into the kitchen. He's holding a newspaper, and the look on his face is one of respect. I'm not quite sure what has him in such a great mood. My only worry is where Morgan is, and if Vyper has made his way back to the Quarter.

"What is it?" I ask, holding out my hand for the paper. As soon as he turns it around and lays it in my hand, I read the headline.

Serial Rapist Found Beaten

"Morgan?" I ask, looking up at him. On his nod, I skim the article and see that the man was found unconscious after a 911 call from a tenant at an apartment complex had found him beside a dumpster while taking out the trash. I chuckled to myself. If this was Morgan's doing, she gave the man what he deserved, dumping him like he'd done several of his victims.

"Looks like something she'd do," Cyrus smiles.

"I wouldn't doubt she got a call in the early morning hours." I smile and shake my head. She's committed to the women in this city.

"I also have information on the Painted Devils and the VP that was murdered," Cyrus says, removing his phone from his pocket. "The man's name was Corin Bradley. His wife, Nancy, was killed the year before…and they have a daughter."

"Morgan?" I ask, feeling my heartbeat faster

in my chest.

"Actually," he begins, handing me his phone. "Her real name is Emily Bradley. She was seventeen when her father was murdered. Her mother was killed the year before when her car ran off the road and into a lake outside of Portland, Oregon."

"Fuck," I groan, seeing a picture of Morgan from a high school yearbook. She couldn't have been more than fifteen years old. She was smiling, and her blue eyes were alight with innocence.

"Duke?"

"He's left the MC," Cyrus replies. "Not sure if he was overthrown or he left, but he's no longer with them. I did find out that he's been in Baton Rouge working at Sandlot's as a bouncer for the past two months."

"Son of a bitch!" I roar. "That's how he and Vyper have gotten together."

"Apparently, they've been hanging around each other a lot," Cyrus curses. "I talked to Harvey late last night, and he said word on the streets is Vyper has been staying at Duke's place."

"And we know where that is, right?" I push. I need to end both of these men before they come after Morgan.

"Rocco and Moose are already on their way to

Baton Rouge to find them," Cyrus promises, but shakes his head in defeat. "No one, not even Harvey, knows where Duke is staying."

"I want a report from them every few hours," I order, slapping the paper on the counter. "Right now, I need to get to Morgan to make sure she wasn't hurt last night. Have Lola meet with the liquor distributor."

"The car is waiting outside," he says as he heads toward the door. "I'll ride with you."

"Let's go."

Our first stop is her apartment. Where she lives in the Quarter, there is a small wrought iron gate on the left side of the building that holds the noisy restaurant. The gate is rusty, but the deadbolt on the door is solid. It looks as if it's been replaced recently, but I know that my man can get us in.

"Give me less than five minutes," Cyrus says as he checks his surroundings. I hear his tools as they work to pick the lock. A man on a bicycle passes but doesn't pay us any attention. I heard the lock release and I hurry up the stairs to the second-floor apartment. There is only one door at the top of the stairs. I raise my knuckles to the wooden frame and knock loudly. "Morgan!"

Nothing. No sounds, no answer. She is either

out of the building or she's unconscious. "Pick this one, too."

Cyrus hurries and pops the lock, pushing the door open wide. I am shocked at what I see. There is absolutely nothing in the apartment to indicate she lives here.

The walls are painted a dark beige, and the living room only holds a couch that looks like it should've been thrown out a decade ago. She has a small television and a coffee table. The kitchen is clean, but the counters are bowed and sunken in. I look toward a bathroom and another room off the living room.

"She doesn't seem like the type to live in this shithole." Cyrus cringes when he sits on her couch. He moves to his left and pokes at a hole in the cushion.

"She shouldn't be living here," I curse, walking around her apartment to look for any sign that she's been here. After a long inspection and only finding some clothes and toiletries, I follow Cyrus back to the car after locking up everything the way I'd found it.

We spend all morning and afternoon hunting for Morgan. Cyrus stays glued to the internet for any reports of activity that has her calling card. I'm pissed when there are none. I don't know where she is or who has her, and my mind automatically thinks that Vyper *and* Duke have her locked in a dungeon somewhere.

We stop at the warehouse in Hammond. My shipment of construction supplies has arrived, and I order the men to get everything separated and ready to deliver to the companies who've placed orders for the product.

"So, we're in the construction supply business now?" Cyrus heaves a sigh, and I can see the numbers he's calculating in his head. It's not as profitable as my less than legal jobs.

"It's a legit company." I nod toward the product. "It won't make as much money as the powder coming in from Mexico, but it'll keep us out of jail."

"So, you're serious about this change?"

"I am," I reply.

"Whatever you want." He pauses, looking over the pallets of materials. "I'm right behind you."

"Thank you." I return to the SUV and sit in the backseat, checking my phone for any messages from my men. Morgan still hasn't been found, and the little huntress is worrying me. I call her phone for the eleventh time since I woke up. There is no answer.

Cyrus answers a phone call and stands outside of the SUV for several minutes. He slips the phone into his pocket and slides into the driver's side. He doesn't pull away, and I look at him through the rearview mirror. "What?"

"Rocco has a problem with one of your suppliers," he says, narrowing his eyes. "This is something you need to deal with if you want out of that business."

"Tell me," I snarl.

"Victor Mendez owes you a ton of money," Cyrus begins. "When Rocco stopped by to collect, Victor was acting weird. After a bit of encouragement, he admitted that he blew the money at the casino."

"*All of it?*" I yell, my anger and the darkness boiling just under my skin. If this son of a bitch is still breathing when we get there, I will end him. He owes me over a hundred grand.

"All of it," Cyrus confirms.

"Take me to him," I order, and sit back in my seat. Cyrus takes off and heads back toward the Quarter. I need to take care of one more problem before I concentrate my efforts on finding the huntress.

Chapter 24
Morgan

Anger sends my blood pressure into dangerous territory. With my binoculars, I can see the two men standing outside of the tattoo parlor. Vyper is smoking a cigarette while Duke is on the phone. He looks like he is irritated, and Vyper raises a brow when Duke throws his hands in the air. Whatever he's being told on the other end of the line irritates him.

I have several hours before darkness falls and I can plan my move. I've never gone after two men at once, and I'm nervous. Seeing Duke has brought back so many memories from my youth. I can't let those thoughts hinder my attack. Letting that bullshit in could destroy me…for good this time.

A car drives by the tattoo parlor, and it looks familiar. The windows are heavily tinted, and I know it's one of Jackson's men. Vyper narrows his eyes as it passes and throws his cigarette to the ground. He slips down the side of the building and around the back. Less than a minute later, he leaves in a black SUV.

I slide behind the wheel of my car and pull out onto the road. Vyper is driving fast in the opposite direction of Jackson's men, and makes a turn on the interstate, heading north. I pass a silver Volvo and press down on the gas, sliding back into the right lane with little room to spare before I have to take the ramp.

My hand slams on the steering wheel when I get caught between several tractor trailers. I can barely see his taillights up ahead, and as soon as the traffic up ahead clears, Vyper shoots off at a high rate of speed. I've lost him. "Fuck!"

I take the next exit and get back on the highway, heading south. I'll return to my apartment until tomorrow night. I have no doubt I'll catch them at some point now that I know where they're hiding. Now that I've found Vyper, it won't take long for me to get him alone. After that, he will be done.

I park on the street and start to step out of my vehicle, but I narrow my eyes when I see a tinted SUV across the street. I know it's Jackson.

I can't see him, but my eyes stare at the back window as I wait. I can feel him around me even though there is no contact. Memories from the night I spent in his bed swim through my head like an out of control train and I shiver.

The interior light comes on when the driver's side door opens. A dark-skinned man steps out and adjusts his suit jacket. He doesn't look at me as he opens the rear door. Black denim covered legs drop to the ground only seconds before Jackson steps around the open door. He looks angry; the hard set to his jaw gives him away. He crosses the street and reaches for the handle of my door, yanking it open roughly.

"What the fuck were you doing going to Baton Rouge without help?" He's angry. I can feel the tension radiating off of him, and I want nothing more than to wallow in it. I want him to kiss me for being so stubborn, but I don't show him how much his anger affects me in this way.

"I don't need backup," I breathe out, swallowing hard when his eyes narrow. "I…"

His lips cover my mouth, and any retort I can throw at him is silenced. He tastes of whiskey and anger. My hand grabs his shirt over his heart and I make a tight fist, holding him hostage where he stands. God, I want him to yell at me again. I want to see the emotions in his eyes.

"I've been looking for you all fucking day, Morgan," he growls as he leans back to catch a breath. Jackson Pace doesn't let me speak before he kisses me silent yet again. It takes several minutes of his lips against mine before he releases me. "You are staying with me."

"I'm staying at my apartment tonight," I pant, feeling out of breath from his punishment.

"Scoot over," he demands. I open my eyes wide and start to shake my head, but he cuts me off before I can protest. "Right now is not the time to piss me off."

"I'll drive," I smirk, knowing he isn't going to hurt me. He's angry and needs to be brought down a notch. "You can sit in the passenger side and stew."

"You like testing me?" he snarls, not moving from his spot at my door.

"Yes," I grin and push him away, closing my door as soon as he is clear. I hear his vicious curse as he rounds my car. Jackson Pace doesn't like being told what to do. Well, he doesn't know me very well.

"I should take you across my knee," he says as he closes his door. Before I can reply, his lips are on mine again, and I drown in his darkness. It is there in every bite, strong hand hold on my hair, my neck, my chin, and the heavy breath he takes as soon as he's determined he is done kissing me. When Jackson pulls back, I see a splash of red on his collar and I fist his shirt in my hand, pulling the material closer for my inspection.

"Blood?"

"I had to deal with a problem today." He shrugs and leans back in his seat. "Drive, Morgan. I'm in no mood for small talk."

"Fine," I snap, pulling away from the curb.

Chapter 25

Jackson

Her defiance makes my cock hard, and I want nothing more than to take her to my room to show her how much it affects me.

"So, you found him?" I push, knowing she was there in Baton Rouge, spying on my man.

"I found them both," she says, taking a deep breath. "I will go back in a few days to finish them off."

"I'm sending my men in to get them tonight," I state, reaching out to grab the door handle when she slams on the brakes and pulls over to the curb.

"The fuck you are, Jackson!"

"Morgan," I growl. "This isn't up for discussion."

"Get out," she demands, pointing toward the

sidewalk. When I don't budge, her eyes narrow and before she can yell at me again, I kiss her lips to shut her up. "Stop! You can't kiss me every single time I don't listen to you."

"It's either I kiss you or I'm going to kill one of my men because I'm so pissed at you," I warn, knowing I would never take my anger out on her.

"You wouldn't." She scrunches her eyes and points toward the curb again. "Get out of my car, Jackson. I just want to go back to my apartment for the night."

I know she's lying. Morgan is going to go back to Baton Rouge and settle the hit that's been put out on Vyper and possibly take down the man who violated her all those years ago. I need to make sure she doesn't get caught by them. The thought of Vyper harming her sends me back to the dark place I don't care to be in when she is with me.

"You are not to go after them yet," I order, hoping she will listen to me. "You are to listen to what I tell you, and I'm telling you it's dangerous to go at both of them alone."

"All I need is two bullets," she responds.

"A bullet for Vyper, yes." I sigh heavily. "You want to torture Duke for the things he's done to you, and don't lie to me...I know you more than you think. You have a darkness inside you as deep as my own."

"I want him to suffer." She pauses to swallow hard. "He deserves it."

"A quick death isn't punishment enough," I agree.

"Jackson," she says, then pauses. By the look in her eyes, I already know the words that are going to come out of her mouth before they are even spoken. "I need you to get out of my car."

"Morgan." I say her name with warning, but she just shakes her head. I don't even see her hand move before she raises her gun, pressing it to my forehead in the confines of the car.

"Get. Out!" I raise my hands to show her I won't fight her. She's determined to go at this alone.

"You don't have to do this alone," I remind her, but reach for the handle when he pushes the gun further into my head. "Fine. I'll leave, but I'll be close."

"Goodbye, Jackson," she whispers. As I climb out of the car, I see a lone tear roll down her face.

Chapter 26
Morgan

Light filters through my blinds, signaling another day has dawned. I don't dare move as I listen for sounds in my apartment. There is a hint of Jackson's cologne in the air, and in my sleep-clogged brain, I remember the night the week before when he tried to kiss me into submission.

I can't think about him right now. Two nights ago, Brooke's mother called to say that the young girl was out of the hospital and they were taking her to New York until Vyper is found. I reassured her that he would be taken care of before the end of the week, and I plan on keeping that promise.

I freeze when I hear a rustle of clothing, forgetting my talk with the mother. My gun is tucked into the cushion of my couch, and my fingers find the cold metal with ease. In a heartbeat, I pull the gun and fall to my knees beside the couch, aiming the weapon at Jackson's stoic face.

"You like holding me at gunpoint, don't you?"

"How did you get in here?" My finger moves away from the trigger and I push the safety on to secure the weapon before lowering it.

"Picked the lock," he says plainly.

"Damnit, Jackson!" I breathe, "I could've shot you!"

"But you didn't," he answers, standing up from his seat at my small kitchen table. "I'm taking you out of this shithole apartment, Morgan…or should I call you Emily?"

"Fuck," I curse in defeat. He's found out who I really am, and I can't lie to him anymore. He knows who Duke is and traced that back to my father. "I'm not Emily anymore, Jax."

"We need to talk about this," he says, extending his hand to help me up from my position on the floor. I accept and stand, turning to the side to place my gun at the small of my back.

"There's not much to talk about that you probably don't already know," I mumble, walking over to start a pot of coffee. I look at the clock above my stove and realize it's only seven in the morning. I slept for four hours, and the yawn I produce gives it away. "When did you get here?"

"Just after six," he replies.

"Roman was across the street in a vehicle when I arrived home early this morning." I pour both of us a cup of coffee and hand his over, remembering he likes his black. "He was still there when I laid down."

"He's still out there." Jackson nods toward the window. "Did you have another client last night?"

"I did," I say, picking up my phone and ignore the bruises on my knuckles. I scroll through the news feeds and find the article where the man was taken into custody. I turn the phone around for Jackson to see. He takes it out of my hand and reads the article in its entirety. After he is done, I notice his jaw tic. He's gauging his words, but I don't need to guess what he's here to say. "Spit it out, Jackson. I know you want to say something."

"It's been a week since you kicked me out of your car, Morgan," he states, bringing up the elephant in the room. "You also missed your appointment with the doc to have your stitches removed."

"I had them removed." I see red creep up his cheeks, and I know he is angry. Landry took out my stitches two nights ago. He didn't question me anymore as to my dealings with Jackson Pace, and I'm glad my old friend didn't snoop.

"Where's Vyper and Duke?" he asks. The hard set to his jaw tells me he knows the two men have gone missing.

"I can't find them," I admit. "I've looked everywhere."

"Another reason why I need to take you back to my place," he says, looking around my tiny space. "Your apartment isn't safe enough."

"It is," I disagree.

"Do not argue with me, Morgan," he barks, setting his cup on the counter as he approaches. His hips press against mine as he takes my chin between his thumb and forefinger. I see the darkness in his eyes as he leans closer. "I know you like it when I get angry. I can tell by the way your body responds to me. You are going to come to the club with me until we find them both, and you will not disobey me this time. Are we clear?"

"I can take care of myself," I remind him, shifting my weight to ease the ache between my legs. I like it when he throws his power at me, and I should be disgusted, but I'm not.

"I know you can," he smirks, knowing I'm going to leave with him regardless. "Gather your things. I'd like to return to the club and get some sleep before the night begins."

He presses his lips to mine and releases me to let me pass. I want to slap him again, but I resist. Jackson is right. I will listen to him and return to the club without issue. His concern for me makes me uncomfortable. I've never had a man in my life who worries for my safety.

"Jackson…" I pause at the threshold to my bedroom. When he raises a brow in response, I speak the words that I have been going over in my head for the past week. "Your concern for me is frightening, and I don't know how to react."

"You are mine, Morgan Rayne, and that's all you need to worry about."

Chapter 27
Jackson

My mood is lighter as we reach Club Phoenix. Roman holds the back door open to allow us to pass. The music in the bar is at a softer volume for this early in the morning. There are still several hours before the customers will start arriving and the night will get going. We are expecting a larger than normal crowd seeing as the weather has started cooling off and it is Friday night.

"Hungry?" I inquire. She looks tired and from watching her sleep for an hour, I know she was restless in her slumber.

"Actually," she nods, pausing to touch her flat stomach, "I am."

"I'll make us something," I offer as we climb the stairs. Roman follows us silently and makes his excuse as he reaches the top of the stairs. There is a small, two-bedroom apartment behind the bar that I've left furnished for my employees to use.

"I didn't know he lived here," Morgan observes as she watches Roman exit through a door next to the one that leads to my living quarters.

"He doesn't," I clarify, pushing open my door. I walk toward the small kitchen and open the fridge. I remove eggs and bacon, thinking I'll make a quick, hearty meal for the both of us before we take a nap. "I have that for my employees to use if they stay late at the club. It's a two-bedroom apartment with a bath. There is a small kitchen set up for them to use as well."

"I heard Vyper was living here," she states as she takes a seat on a barstool at the island. Who has she been talking to? Someone in this city is working with her, and I'm going to find out who it is. If it's one of my people, they won't be working for me for long. No one is to speak about my affairs without my permission. Even though it's Morgan who found out that Vyper was staying here, the fact they gave out the information makes them guilty in my book.

"He was," I nod. "The bastard fled without taking his things the night the woman was hurt." I don't go into details about what he left behind. I was shocked at the things I found in his room. Only Cyrus, Roman, and I are privy to the items we removed from the bedroom. Vyper had certain tastes in his pleasures, and none of them were sane.

"Brooke," she corrects me with a scowl on her face. "Her name is Brooke."

"I'm sorry?" I say, setting down the spatula and walking around the bar to pull her into my arms.

"They all have names," she continues, not releasing me. I take that as a good sign. I've obviously upset her for being so withdrawn.

"I know they do, and I apologize again for being so thoughtless," I say, pressing a kiss to her forehead.

"It's okay," she sighs, running her finger under the hair tie on her wrist. I don't stop her and move away to continue making us something to eat. "I didn't peg you as a cook."

"I have many talents," I tease, handing over her plate. After I take a seat, she begins to eat, and I find myself watching her with fascination. She's very well-mannered and I find that odd, coming from a woman who was raised around a bunch of bikers.

"I'm sure you do," she blushes. The hardened features of the huntress are gone, and I find myself needing more information to understand her better.

There are so many conflicting things about this woman, and I fear I may never know who she truly is.

"Tell me about your father," I say as we sit down to eat. I narrow my eyes when Morgan's fork pauses halfway to her lips. She sets it down hard on her plate and swings her narrowed gaze in my direction.

"He's dead," she snarls.

"There's something else that ties Duke into all of this," I push. "There are things you are not telling me. Why did your father let that man harm you?"

"I don't want to discuss this," she says, fisting her hands on the top of the bar. "I've buried the past, Jackson. Why can't you accept that?"

"So, you're just going to ignore that the man who violated you is close enough to hurt you again?" I curse and slam my hand next to the plate, causing Morgan to jolt from my anger. I don't even apologize when I push the stool back and take my plate to the sink, not even bothering to scrap off the remaining food.

"I will find him my way," she growls, rising to her feet. "You have got to stop coddling me, Jackson. This is the very reason why I work alone. I cannot have someone care for me. It's too dangerous. People get hurt when they are close to me."

"The only person getting hurt is Vyper and Duke," I promise, turning around to point at her. "You are mine, and I will lock you in this apartment until I find them to keep you safe."

"Fuck you, Jax," she snarls, pivoting on her heel. My eyes track her moving toward the door, and the darkness inside me flares when I realize she's leaving me again.

"You are not leaving here until you tell me what happened between you, your father, and Duke," I demand, slamming my hand on the door to my apartment as soon as she opens it. The echo of the force rattles the photos on the wall.

"My father sold me to Duke." She curses and spins around. My arms have her caged in, and I don't move. Her admission breaks open the crust that holds my demons deep inside, allowing them to climb out of their cages.

"*He did what?*" I bellow, panting hard.

"Duke owns me," she explains. "He won't stop until he has me, Jackson. It's best that I leave. I cannot bring anyone else into this, especially not you. It is my problem to deal with, and his death must be by my hands, and my hands alone."

"Sit down on the couch," I whisper, looking toward the ground. My hands are still on the door, and Morgan remains caged there. She doesn't move right away, and I drop one hand to my side. "Get away from the door."

She must sense my anger and finally obeys. I don't even look at her as I pull the door open and start to head down to my office, knowing Cyrus is there waiting for me. Morgan curses and beats on the door when I lock her inside. I rest my head against the wood and whisper, "I have to protect you. You are my world now, Morgan Rayne."

"Find Vyper and Duke," I demand as soon as I see my man. My teeth are clenched so tight, I fear they will break from how tight my jaw is clamped. "I want them brought to me."

Chapter 28
Morgan

Jackson leaves me alone in his apartment, and I hear the lock engage as soon as he closes the door. The man wasn't kidding when he threatened to keep me locked up for my safety.

"You asshole!" I scream as I beat my fist on the door. I know what he has planned, and I can't let him go after Duke. The man is far too dangerous.

I put my phone to my ear and call Landry. He answers on the first ring, "Hello, Morgan?"

"Jackson Pace has locked me in his fucking castle to keep me from going after Vyper and Duke."

"You cannot go after both of them alone, and you know it, Morgan," he scolds.

"I have to be the one to end this, Landry." I pace the floor in front of the door, hoping that maybe, just maybe, Jackson will have a change of heart and return soon.

"It'll be the last hunt you ever complete," he says. "I'm warning you, Morgan. Don't rush into this without help from Jackson."

"I'm…I'm sorry, Landry," I sigh, resigning myself to not listen to him. "I have to go."

"Morgan…" I hang up the phone and tuck it in the back pocket of my shorts.

I check the windows and finally find one I can safely climb from to reach the fire escape. I don't even bother closing the window when I leave. It takes only seconds for my feet to hit the ground behind the dumpster next to the kitchen door to the bar. Thankfully, no one is lingering out back at this time of the morning. I hurry down the back alley and come out at a busy intersection. I check my surroundings and breathe a sigh of relief that I haven't been followed by Jackson or his men.

At my apartment, I grab my car keys and prepare to head out. I make sure all of my belongings are hidden in the wall safe behind my dresser. I make it out of my building without problems, and I know it's only a matter of minutes before Jackson realizes I am gone.

He cannot be involved with Duke and his

death. I wasn't lying to him when I said the man was mine to kill. There is a haunting need to spill his blood for the things he's done to me. Now that I know where both men are, I will take them out at once. A bullet to Vyper's head will be sufficient enough, but Duke will stay alive a while longer. I need to make him suffer.

I drive with caution as I leave the Quarter and head toward Baton Rouge. My phone rings in the passenger seat, but I ignore it when I see Jackson's number flash across the screen. After the third time he calls, I power down the phone and drop it in the center console. I cannot have his distractions or his demands. I have to go at this alone.

I arrive at the bar called Sandlot's after driving around town to kill some time. I get there right as the sun is setting. There are only a handful of cars in the lot, and I decide to make myself known. I know what I'm doing is dangerous, but I'm done with waiting to take out Vyper. If I have to put a bullet in his head at the bar, so be it. I have ways of running, and I'm good at it, because I've been doing it for years.

The inside of the bar is more like a restaurant with booths. There is a long bar top to my left, and a young waitress tells me to take a seat anywhere in the place. I move to the back booth next to the emergency exit and ask for a shot of liquid courage.

"Double shot of tequila, cold," I say, picking up the menu I will not order from. The thought of food sours my stomach.

The waitress returns and sets down my drink with a glass of ice water. I push it aside and take my shot. The moment my eyes level out, I see Vyper. He comes in the front door and stops at the end of the bar. A beer is slid over to him as he takes a seat.

My fingers twitch as I roll the empty glass between them. I want that man dead, and by the end of the night, he will be mine. I need to know where Duke is so I can keep them separated. Jackson was right. I cannot take them both on at the same time.

If it'd been any other man, I could use my looks to lure him out of the club. I'm sure that Vyper knows who I am and what I look like since Duke has been hanging around. If I play anything but my best hand, I will fail.

Vyper finishes his beer and heads to the door as a few men enter. He checks their ID's and allows them to pass. The music changes into something a little heavier and louder, and several men head to a pool table by the large front window.

"Another drink?" the waitress asks.

"Please," I reply, only glancing at her for a second.

Vyper hasn't noticed me yet, and I keep to my seat in the darkened booth. I know that Jackson's men have got to be close. He would've immediately sent them to this location the moment he found me missing from his apartment. The hard shell around my heart cracks just a little more when I think about how I left him to come to Baton Rouge, but I cannot let it hinder my task. I'll think about Jackson Pace and my feelings for him once this is all over.

A shot glass is set in front of me and I nod my thanks to the waitress. She doesn't speak as she walks away. I take the shot and remove money from my pocket to drop on the table.

It's time for me to duck out the back door. I've been here too long, and I need to find where Duke is hiding. I remember seeing an old motel a few blocks away. I wouldn't put it past these two to have a room there.

The side door is not locked as I push it open, and I make my escape. My car is parked close, and I slide behind the wheel quickly. There are no cars in the lot that would make me think Jackson is close by, but that doesn't mean he isn't here.

I pull out on the street that leads toward the

motel. It only takes me two minutes to arrive, and I park in front of the office. When I enter the building, an old man is sitting behind a glass window, reading a newspaper.

"I need a room for the night," I say, sliding over a hundred dollar bill. He doesn't question me or even ask for a driver's license. The man just drops a key onto the counter and pushes it through a small opening, mumbling, "Check out is at noon."

Thankfully, the room is on the backside of the building and my car will be hidden from the street. I don't see the SUV Vyper was driving the other night, but that doesn't mean anything. I remove my gun from the holster in my boot and tuck it at the small of my back, covering it with my plaid, button-down shirt.

The outside light over the door is burned out, and it is pitch black on the sidewalk in front of the door. I take stock of the corners of the building and the one dim light across the lot, finding no cameras in sight. Again, there are no darkly tinted cars or SUVs around, and I take that as a good sign Jackson doesn't know where I am. Now that my car is stashed out of sight from the road, I stick to the darker areas of the lot to make my way back toward the bar. The walk shouldn't take me more than five minutes.

My goal is to be lying in wait when Vyper leaves the bar tonight. I can take him out in the parking lot and be back to my room before the cops show up to investigate. With the light being out over the door to my room, I can slip back inside without being seen.

The photos of Brooke in the hospital filter through my mind's eye as I wait. No one should have to go through the things she had on that night. Vyper is one of the worst monsters out there. Just like Duke, the man is sick in so many ways.

The sign in the window by the door showing the bar is open flickers and fades out as the bar begins to close. Several patrons spill out and I see Vyper holding the door open as they pass. Bile rises in my mouth when a young, blonde woman stumbles out and his eyes rake her with lust. I want to kill him twice now.

One by one, the cars leave and eventually the lot clears. I'm standing behind a thick bush a few feet from an SUV, and I assume it's one of the employee's vehicles. I take it as a good sign that Duke hasn't been around. This will make my job much easier.

I sink low into the darkness when Vyper exits the building and starts walking toward me. I'm silent, not even breathing as he gets closer. There are no cars driving past, and no one else has come out. Now is my time.

I reach for my gun, but a heavy hand wraps around my wrist…another around my mouth. A voice from my past chuckles in my ear as I am jerked against a large body.

"Well, hello, Emily," Duke says, as his nose traces my neck and I shiver from the memories. "I've missed you."

"I'm not Emily anymore," I snarl, slamming my head back. I hear the crack of his nose on impact. The son of a bitch doesn't let me go, and I feel fear for the first time in seven years when Vyper looks up and sees us scuffling in the shadows.

"The Huntress?" Vyper asks as he approaches.

"That's what I hear," Duke laughs as he tightens his hold. It's nothing more than a game for these two. "When I'm done with her, she will be my old lady until I use her up."

"Hmm," Vyper smiles, his gray eyes darkening. "I'd love to play with her when you're done."

"Not fucking happening," I bark, using the leverage of Duke's hold to kick out, twisting until my boot makes contact with Vyper's jaw.

"You bitch!" Vyper comes at me as Duke hooks his leg around my ankle. We fall to a heap on the ground and I scramble to get out from underneath them both. My gun is missing, but I'm smaller than they are. I try to use that to my advantage to go after Vyper as he stands up to brush himself off like I was nothing more than an annoying fly. It only takes Duke's deep baritone voice to freeze me in my tracks.

"If you don't stop fighting, we will kill Jackson."

A phone is shoved in my face, and on the live video, I see a the hand of a person driving behind Jackson's SUV with a gun trained on the back window.

"Jackson has men looking for you," I remind him, acting unfazed, but on the inside, I am screaming for Jackson to duck. I care for him, and that realization strikes me like a blow to the chest. I can't let them think their threats mean anything to me. "Even if you do kill him, the others will come for you."

"I don't think so," Vyper laughs as he wipes blood from his lip. I have a small amount of satisfaction from being the one to make the first hit.

"You will be going back to Oregon with me," Duke says, jerking my arm so he can hold me tight against his chest again. He flips the phone around to face Vyper. "Tell them to take the shot."

"No!" I scream as I hear three shots fire from the speaker on the phone. A second later, the screen goes black. "You son of a bitch!"

"Time to punish you for leaving me," Duke says, bringing my own gun down at an angle. Pain flares in my head as everything goes dark.

Chapter 29
Jackson

Duke and Vyper took the bait. There is no question about where Morgan went when she escaped from my apartment at the club. We knew she was going to Baton Rouge alone, but it's confirmed when my cell phone rings with an unknown number.

"Who is this?" I bark into the phone as a way of a greeting.

"Landry Pierre," the man says over the line. I know who he is but have never had the pleasure of meeting the old man who knows all in the Quarter. He's known for being a plethora of information on the underground.

"What can I do for you, sir?" Landry is like the Godfather. Respect is earned, and this man is shown the highest.

"If you care for Morgan, go get her now," he says. "That girl is like a daughter to me, and I want you to bring her home."

"Yes, sir." I pause. "She's quite stubborn."

"Dat she is," he chuckles. The man is a native, and his Cajun drawl is proof to his roots here in Louisiana. "She's hell bent on her task, but this one may be too much."

"That's what I've been telling her." My voice sounds tired, and I hear him chuckle under his breath. "I'll bring her home tonight."

"Goodnight, Mr. Pace."

"Thank you, Mr. Pierre."

I arm all of my men, and we leave in three separate vehicles within ten minutes of the call from Landry Pierre. Keon is waiting with the motor running as I slide into the backseat. Roman jumps in the passenger side of the car in front of me and we leave the Quarter as fast as possible.

A tinted, older model BMW falls in behind us when we are twenty minutes away from the bar. The three shots they get off don't do anything more than bounce off the glass of the SUV. I'm smarter than they think. Bulletproof glass is expensive, but well worth the cost if it keeps me from bleeding out on the leather seats.

"Hang on, Jackson," Keon says from the front seat.

The vehicle jerks forward and we rocket off down the street, leaving them in our wake. My driver takes a sharp right onto a side street, and I twist around in my seat to see the car miss the turn. We are several blocks away when Keon turns back onto the highway.

"I think we've lost them," he growls. "That was too fucking close, Jackson."

"I know." My phone rings and I answer it on the first ring. "Roman?"

"We have an address where her car is parked," he informs me. He texts the location and warns, "Do not go after her until we get there."

"Hurry," I say, ending the call. Keon advises me we are less than ten minutes away when I hand him my phone.

If they've harmed one hair on her head, I will torture them with no remorse. The darkness inside of me cannot be held at bay anymore. Vyper has threatened what is mine, and I will make him suffer every waking moment he has left.

Chapter 30
Morgan

"You're a pussy," I goad the moment I wake up with a headache from being knocked out. Both men are standing over me as they have me tied to the nasty hotel bed. I am naked, and I look down at my body to see what has been done to me while I was out. Thankfully, Duke hadn't cut me like he did all those years ago. I am unharmed...for now. I have no doubt he will do worse things to me than he did all those years ago.

"I should cut out your tongue," Duke warns as he kneels on the bed and presses a knife to my throat.

"Do it," I laugh, pulling at my restraints. Unlike when Jackson caught me, these knots are exposed. So, any attempt to get out will be seen by them. I will have to wait until they are otherwise occupied, but at the moment, I don't think they have anywhere to go.

Duke backhands me instead. I laugh loudly. "You hit like a girl."

"Duke!" Vyper warns when the man who turned me into a killer comes at me again. Duke recovers himself, and I frown. Why would these two men hold back from hurting me? Unless?

"Are you using me to get to Jackson?" I ask, seeing Vyper pause as he turns to walk away. Where does Duke fit into this mission?

"Jackson Pace should be dead by now," Duke boasts. "I'm just here to get what's mine."

"I'm not yours," I remind him. Vyper is off standing by a small table that sits in the corner. He's very intently focused on whatever he's fiddling with and ignoring us. I hear the *tap, tap, scrap* of something. When the man leans over, I see him snort a huge line of cocaine. *Fuck.*

"I beg to differ," he replies. "I bought you from your piece of shit father."

"Bought me?" I laugh, pulling at my restraints in hope that they give…they don't. "Bought me? What is this, the middle ages? You're fucking pathetic if you think for one second that you *own* me."

"Let me explain," Duke smirks. I try to pull away when he straddles my body, sitting down hard across my pelvis. The denim of his jeans scratches the tops of my hips, and I try to buck him off, but the cold press of the blade on my skin makes me pause. "You will not fight me, or I will carve you again."

"Fuck you, Duke," I snarl, spitting in his face. He recovers and backhands me again. My mouth will get me killed, but at this point, it's better than being taken back to Oregon. "You better fucking kill me, because I refuse to go back with you. I will cut off your cock when you sleep, and when you wake up screaming from the pain, I will make you choke on it."

"The way you choked on my cock with your virgin mouth?"

"You liked my bite," I counter. His hand reaches out, wrapping around my throat as he leans in close to my ear. When he does, I feel the ridge of his hard cock against my stomach. I grit my teeth when the knife in his other hand slices my jawline. I refuse to cry. I refuse to beg. Like I said, he's going to have to kill me.

"You've gotten tougher since the last time I saw you." He nods toward Vyper. "This guy has some sick tastes. I bet he can make you scream."

Vyper reaches into a black duffle bag, removing something dark. I can't quite make out what it is until he approaches the bed. My eyes widen, and I hear Duke laugh. I struggle when he wraps the blindfold over my eyes, tying it so tight at the back of my head, I immediately feel the stirrings of a headache.

This isn't good. Without my sight, I don't know what they will do to me. It's a form of torture, and I'm now afraid I will go insane before he kills me. I should've known Duke would get off on this…just like he did when I was younger.

This is it…my nightmares are coming back to life. I feel their hands on me, touching me…holding me in their tight grasps. The sharp bite of the blade cutting into the existing scars on my abdomen sends me screaming into the darkness.

Vyper's excited laugh tells me I am in deeper trouble than I ever thought possible.

Chapter 31
Jackson

Night is within an hour of becoming day, and I've had enough of waiting. I've heard her scream twice in the last twenty minutes, and my men have had to hold me back from rushing the door. I know we need to separate the two men, and I know not to rush into a situation blindly, but I can't hold back much longer. My mind has conjured up all sorts of morbid things that they've done to her, and I don't know what I'm going to find when we enter that room.

"I want them both alive," I growl the moment Vyper steps out of the room. He lights a cigarette and looks at his hands. A sound rips from my throat when I see dried blood on them.

"Jackson, no!" Cyrus warns, but it's too late. My feet begin to march as I round the back of my

SUV; a gun in my hand. I'm only fifty feet from him when Vyper's eyes raise from the ground. I see a moment of fear in them, and that's all I need.

"Where. Is. Morgan?" He doesn't even try to run as I walk right up to him and press the barrel right between his eyes. I can feel Cyrus, Roman, Rocco, and Moose behind me as I press the gun so hard into his head that the man falls to his knees when I force it downward. His eyes are wild, and I'm sure he's on some type of drug…probably cocaine.

"She's spending time with the man who claims her," Vyper laughs. "She's already ruined for you."

"Fuck you," I snarl. I nail him in the jaw with my fist, stepping away when Moose comes forward. Rocco secures Vyper's arms and cuffs him as he lays on the ground. "Take him to my house."

I have no time to say anything else when I hear her voice. It only takes one well-placed kick to the hotel door for it to burst open. The sight before me calls forth the demon who rules my darkness.

"Jackson!" she screams when I enter the room.

My body launches at the man standing inside the door, taking him down. I hear Morgan cursing for all she's worth, but my mind is solely focused on disabling Duke. I nail him in the face once, twice, and on the third strike, blood sprays from his nose. I hit him three more times before he goes limp beneath me. I have his blood all over my hands, and I want to draw more. This is the man who brutalized Morgan when she was just a young girl. She was innocent until he made her into a hardened killer.

"Jackson," she calls out again. "Please…" I hear a hiccup and my head jerks to the side. A roar bubbles out of my throat like I am the monster when I see her tied to the bed. She is naked and has gashes all over her beautiful body. The scars on her belly have been cut open again.

"Morgan," I gasp and climb on the bed. The ropes around her wrists are so tight, her hands have turned blue. I pull the knife from my back pocket and flip open the blade. She jerks slightly but doesn't shy away from me when I cut her free.

"I want to kill him," she breathes as I tuck her safely against my chest. I pull the fitted sheet free from the bed and wrap her up as someone cuts her legs free. All I can think about at the moment is getting her to safety and away from these men. "Please let me kill him."

"You will." That's the only words I can form at the moment.

Keon has the SUV running as I exit the room. We climb in the backseat and the vehicle speeds off toward my home. I cannot think straight enough to do anything other than hold her. I'm hoping one of my men has called the doc.

"Thank you," she whispers. "Thank you."

"Shhh," I respond, and hold her as we head toward home.

"You were right," she cries. "You were right…I couldn't take them both. I failed."

"You didn't fail, baby," I promise, holding her tighter to my chest. "You survived."

"I love you, Jackson," she mumbles. I shake my head because I don't know if I'm hearing her correctly.

"Morgan?"

"I said, 'I love you,'" she repeats, nuzzling into my neck like a kitten seeking warmth. She yawns, and I kiss the top of her head.

"I never thought I'd find someone who could match me…someone who would ever understand my darkness, but I found her." I swallow the lump in my throat.

"I hope she's pretty," Morgan teases. Even bleeding out, she has a comeback.

"I love you, Morgan Rayne," I say as we

approach my house.

* * *

I remove my jacket and toss it on a metal folding chair outside of the room. The blood that pumps through my veins is thrumming with electricity. The darkness has surfaced, and the need to punish these two men is at the forefront of my mind.

"How's Morgan?" I ask Cyrus through gritted teeth as he enters behind me a few seconds later.

"She's still asleep," he replies, his hand on the door as he awaits my nod. "Doc says she should be out for another hour or so."

"As soon as she is able, Duke is hers and hers alone," I demand. On my nod, Cyrus opens the door without comment, closing me inside with the two men who've harmed my huntress.

"Well, well, well," Vyper snickers. "So, how does that bitch look this morning? I hope you enjoy what's left of her." Vyper is really in no position to talk to me that way. I know he's trying to break through my resolve by acting tough. He can lie all he wants. I already know they didn't violate her. All they did was carve her up like a Thanksgiving turkey, and I will spend all of my money to have her put back together if that's what she wants. My huntress will not suffer anymore.

We are in an outbuilding on my property, and he is mine to punish. This man will pay for the things he did to Brooke, and for aiding in Morgan's capture. There is a drain in the floor and hooks hanging from the ceiling. Vyper is suspended from one and Duke is hanging unconscious from the other. Vyper knows this room well. He's been in here before, but as an employee of mine…not an enemy.

"You have disobeyed me," I begin, removing a six-inch knife from its spot on a small table. It's recently been sharpened, and I take a moment to admire Roman's skills at making the blade gleam.

"My kinks are my own business, not yours," Vyper continues.

"I gave you a warning when I removed your pinky after you left my waitress in an abandoned hotel. You'd choked her to the point of almost killing her while you were balls deep inside her." I walk up to him and press the knife to his jaw and draw it against his skin, slowly cutting him to the bone…just as they'd done to Morgan. "What you did to Brooke goes far beyond a wild fuck. Secondly, the fact that you helped Duke harm Morgan seals your fate."

"She liked it," he laughs, blood trailing down

the column of his throat. "They *both* liked it."

"I saw Brooke's injuries," I admit. "That young woman will be scarred for life because of you."

"Again, she *begged* for it," he snickers, but grunts when my fist lands in the center of his stomach.

"She did not," I reply. Stepping back to where my leather pouch that holds my knives sits on a small table, I don't even look up at Vyper's reaction as I remove one and test its weight on my palm. "You enjoy cutting them, don't you? You get off on torture. Well, let's see how you like it when the tables are turned."

He doesn't speak, and I watch as he begins to sweat. Good, because I'm about to make him bleed. He will bleed for Brooke. He will bleed for Morgan, too. I flip the knife around in my palm until it is facing the way I need it. With one quick slash of my hand, Vyper grunts but doesn't scream when the knife cuts across his abdomen. "This one is for Morgan."

"Fuck you," he snarls, clenching his jaw tight. His sharp teeth are exposed, and I want to cut them out of his fucking mouth for the bite wounds on Brooke's breasts.

"Brooke's legs were fileted open," I snarl as I

lash out on his upper thigh. Vyper doesn't even grunt this time. I repeat the same wound he gave her on his other leg. Blood starts to trickle down his legs. I pick up a much larger knife and slowly walk around behind him.

"What are you doing?" he asks. There is just a hint of panic in his voice, and the darkness inside me craves it.

He screams when I cut the back of one of his knees. "She couldn't even walk."

His body drops but doesn't fall to the ground because of the chains that hold him suspended from the rafters in the building. I look down and watch as the first rivulets of his blood reach the drain in the floor beneath him. By the time I am finished, that drain will have his life inside it.

"Fuck…you," Vyper groans through gritted teeth.

"I should geld you, you son of a bitch," I snarl, feeling the darkness creeping to the surface. My demons are swirling around in my mind. *Take out the threat. Take him out.* "I should dismember you while you're still alive."

"Do it, you fucker!" Vyper is yanking on the chains. He knows his time is coming to an end. The ball is in my court, and I have a choice to make.

Kill him slowly?

Make it quick?

"Do you like the bite of my blade?" I ask, circling him like the wounded animal he is. My demons stir and I wait for his answer. The blood from my cuts is slowly dripping off his feet. His legs are covered in blood.

"You're just as sick and twisted as I am," he taunts.

"I will never be like you. I hope you rot in hell," I snarl, and drive the knife right into his stomach, shoving it upwards into his body. Vyper gasps for breath as I remove the knife, dropping it to the floor. I turn on my heel and walk out the door just as I hear him take his last breath.

He will never harm another woman, and now the ones he's hurt can find closure and move on with their lives.

Chapter 32
Morgan

I fight the sedative, but it always wins. Every time I close my eyes, my past comes back to haunt me. The ditch, the smell of the mud as my fingers dug into the muck…the pain of the violation. All of it rushes back, and I wake up screaming.

Doctor Barnes is there with a needle. The pain is too much right now, and I reluctantly let the doctor knock me out. My only saving grace is that Jackson promises me I am safe. Even if his touch doesn't stop the nightmares.

He smells of cigarettes and beer. The man who runs the motorcycle club with my father always picks me up from school. I have no one else. My mother is dead. I know he killed her or had her killed.

She was nothing to him, and now I am following in her footsteps. He will probably kill me, too.

The sound of his motorcycle sends bile into my mouth. He scares me, but I have to obey. My father will make things worse for me if I don't.

"Come on, little girl," Duke grunts as he drops his cigarette to the ground. "We have plans for tonight."

"Where are we going?" I ask, coming to stand next to him.

"Get on the fucking bike and don't ask questions," he barks, grabbing my arm. I cry out from the pressure of his hold. I don't really have a choice when he yanks me toward his back. I climb on and hold on tightly as he speeds away from the school.

When we approach the clubhouse, I notice my father's bike is there, along with two others that I don't recognize. When we enter the building, he's sitting at a table with two men from other MC's. Why are they here?

"The princess is home," Duke snickers. "Is it done?"

"What's done?" I ask, and immediately regret it when he backhands me. The impact is so hard, I fall to my knees and wipe my lip with the back of my

hand. It's bleeding. I begin to stand, but Duke kicks me in the ribs.

"She's all yours," I hear my father say. "Do whatever you want with her."

"Father? Please don't," I gasp. A pinch registers in the back of my arm, and I look up at Duke to see him capping a syringe. "No..."

I feel him lift me over his shoulder and my body begins to relax. My back hits a mattress and I cannot move, but I know what he's doing. I cry, but no sound escapes me. I fight, but no movements come from my young body. I pray...but no one comes to save me.

I blink and I'm not where I was before. I'm outside. I can't hear any sounds except for the hum of the rain. There are no lights, nothing but a black void. My knees are scuffed up, and most of my clothes are torn away from my body. A pain like no other flairs between my legs, and that's when I remember. Like a bad movie reel, my memories flash back.

A man.

My father's right-hand man.

A needle.

His naked body over my virgin one.

Sleep.

Tears mix with the rain as I feel around for

something solid to hold on to. If I can just find a phone, I can call for help. There's nothing around me but mud and maybe a few limbs. Why is it so dark?

I feel warmth rolling down my arms, my belly, and my face. Why is the cold rain not taking away the warmth? I don't understand.

He must've dumped my body once he was done. Maybe he thinks I'm dead? The various pains in my body are nothing compared to the knowledge that I was tossed out like yesterday's trash after he violated me.

It isn't until I try to climb that I realize that the warmth is from blood...lots of blood. The pain in my belly is almost too much to bear as I try to drag my broken body out of my improvised grave. The scent of the earth rises up and tickles my nose as my fingers dig into the mud for traction.

I try to scream out when lights come around the corner again, but my jaw is frozen in place. It aches, and I just want to cry. I think it's broken. My wrist is surely fractured, my face is swollen, and I don't have the courage to see what damage there is to my abdomen.

I wish my momma was still alive, because I need her right now.

A scream bubbles out of my throat, and I gasp when I wake. My mind scrambles to find an anchor in my fucked up reality. "Where am I?"

"Jackson's home outside the city." Doctor Barnes sits in a chair by the door. His sad smile tells me all I need to know. I'm in bad shape.

"Where's Jackson?"

"He's taking care of business," the doc answers.

"No," I growl, and hiss when pain flares in my belly. I have stitches from what was done to me during my abduction, and they burn when I move. "No, he can't. Vyper is mine!"

The covers tangle in my feet when I try to kick them away. I breathe deep, praying the medicine will quickly leave my body. God, I'm so weak. My eyes flutter close, and I fall back asleep.

Tap

Tap

Scrape

Vyper does a line of cocaine and turns around to glare at my body. I will kill him if he touches me. I will not be violated again. Never…again.

I'd rather die.

The rope is too tight.

Duke straddles my body.

The sharp bite of the cold blade against my jaw.

I scream.

It's dark outside the next time I wake feeling less groggy and more like myself, and I know I've been out most of the day. I don't even bother with shoes when I plant my feet on the cold wood floor. I will not let the nightmares rule me anymore.

Taking a deep breath, I put one foot in front of the other as I stumble to the door. The doctor reaches out for me when I sway, but my hard glare stops him in his tracks. I didn't even know he was in the room.

"What day is it?" I growl, pushing his hands away.

"Thursday," he answers. "You've been home for two days."

"Fuck," I mumble under my breath. The moment I pull the door open, Roman is standing there. His eyes widen and he comes toward me when my body lists to the right.

It's like Jackson has me locked away in the castle again and guards are at every point of entry. Either to protect me from the enemy, or to protect me from myself. I don't know which one it is, but I'm going after Vyper…that is if he's still alive.

"Morgan, you should be in bed," he scolds as his hands latch onto my shoulders, steadying me.

"I need to end this," I demand, feeling a tad bit stronger as my eyes begin to clear. When I look past Roman, I see the other guards waiting in chairs down the hallway. Rocco and Moose immediately stand, and Jackson's driver, Keon, narrows his eyes.

"Let me get Jackson for you," Keon offers as he removes his cell phone from his pocket. He makes a call to Cyrus and tells him I am awake. He nods a few times and hangs up. "Jackson is on his way up. Why don't you sit down before you fall over?"

"Good idea." I give up, sitting in an abandoned chair.

The men shift nervously as they wait on Jackson to appear. It doesn't take long before he rounds the corner, and I know he's been with Vyper, and not from the blood stains on his arms, but by the darkness in his eyes.

"Jackson," I breathe.

"Why are you out of bed?"

"Because I need to finish it," I repeat my earlier ramblings.

"I don't think you are ready for anything," he states, but I push myself upright and face him straight on.

"I…" I can't even gather the strength to argue.

"Get back in the bed," Jackson orders, his eyes darkening. "Duke will be here when you are strong enough."

"I need…" I begin, but my shoulders slump. He's right. I am in no condition to kill a man. I need my strength.

"I will feed you, and you will sleep," Jackson says, scooping me up to return me to the bed. "Rest, baby."

"Is he dead? Is Vyper dead?"

"Yes," Jackson nods. "Brooke's family has been notified."

"Okay," I yawn, my eyes fluttering with my exhaustion. "Okay."

Jackson wakes me later and demands I eat. He's there every time I open my eyes over the next few hours. My body is sore, and I hate feeling so weak. I don't know if I will have the strength tomorrow to deal with Duke, but I force myself to rest so I can end this as soon as possible.

* * *

The sun is high in the sky when I open my eyes, realizing the nightmares have stopped. The sheets next to me are cold, and I know Jackson has been awake for some time. I sigh heavily and push myself upright, surprised at how much stronger I feel.

The door to the bedroom opens and he pauses when he sees me sitting. "How do you feel?"

"Better...stronger," I admit.

"Doc is on his way to check on you," he says, bringing me a cup of coffee. I accept it and take a sip.

"After he leaves, I want to end this," I announce.

"If you're sure."

"I am."

Doctor Barnes arrives and spends about thirty minutes checking me over. He is concerned about me moving around too much with my stitches but agrees to return later in the evening to repair any damage I may do to them when I deal with Duke.

The doctor is as loyal to Jackson as he is his men and gives me the all-clear as he packs up his things. "You call me personally if there is anything you need." He hands me his card, and I take it with a nod.

Jackson stands silently at the end of the bed as he waits for Doctor Barnes to leave. He approaches the bed as the door shuts. "Are you sure?"

"I'm ready," I say, picking up my Glock from

the bedside table. I am too sore to wear jeans to tuck the gun in the waistband. So, I opt for just carrying the gun in my hand. "Let's go."

Jackson reluctantly steps back from the bed, and I can tell he is worried for my safety and well-being. I ignore him and walk past him to the door. As I exit the room, Roman and Cyrus are just coming down the hallway. Both of them stop and stare at me with wide eyes. I'm sure I look like a deranged lunatic as I walk out into the hallway in a tank top and cotton shorts, holding a pistol.

"You up for this?" Roman asks.

"Yes," I reply, my voice strong and sure.

The stitches on my stomach burn as I walk, but I don't show weakness. I can't believe it's been three days since I was saved by Jackson from that hotel room in Baton Rouge. Duke and Vyper were captured, and Vyper has been taken care of while I was sedated. Thankfully, Jackson left Duke for me.

"You don't have to do this today," he says from my side.

"I want it over," I say softly.

Roman walks over to a golf cart, and I'm assuming it's to take us wherever they have Duke. We head to the backyard and down a path toward some trees. The lights from the little vehicle illuminate our way just as the sun is setting. Soon, a building hidden amongst the trees comes into view. Once we stop, Jackson and Roman get off. I take Jackson's hand and stand up slowly. I'm not sure what this building is usually used for, but as soon as I walk in, I know.

"He's in that room." Jackson nods toward a door. I feel his warmth beside me, and I absorb his strength. It's time to bury my demons, starting with the man who took away my innocence. "No one will stop you, and no one will hear you." On the table is a cloth with several knives laid out by size. I take one and tuck it inside the front of my sports bra.

"Thank you," I say through gritted teeth, pushing the door open wide.

Duke is restrained with a chain. The links hang from a hook attached to the exposed beams in this old building that looks as if it'd been used as a small horse stable many years ago. The man doesn't look as tough as he did just three days ago. His left eye is swollen shut, and it appears his cheek is a little scuffed up.

"Take him down," I hear myself say.

At the sound of my voice, Duke stirs. His good eye blinks slowly as he lifts his head. The man who stars in my nightmares smirks slowly. "Come to finish me off?"

"Yes," I reply, not giving any other words. He doesn't deserve them. Roman releases him, but Dukes hands are still tied. "Release his hands."

"Morgan," Jackson warns behind me. He doesn't need to remind me that I am not at my full strength. I know this, but it doesn't matter. I will end Duke today. It can't go on any longer.

"Leave me," I say, my eyes never leaving Duke.

"Morgan," Jackson repeats. I ignore him and nod for Roman to continue.

"Trouble in paradise?" Duke chuckles, looking around me to glare at Jackson. "How's she in bed? Does she whimper when you fuck her?"

Jackson's roar echoes in the building, but I spin on my heel and place my hand on his chest when he tries to go after Duke. "He's saying those things on purpose. Ignore him and leave me alone."

"I cannot leave you in this room alone with him," he whispers, shaking his head as if to clear an image.

"I will be fine," I promise. My words are for him. He has to feel I have control of the situation to let me go at this alone. This is something I've learned about Jackson Pace. He cares too much, but he also respects my strength. If he thought I couldn't handle this, he wouldn't have let me leave the house.

"You are my world, Morgan Rayne," he admits, cupping my face. He doesn't kiss me, and I am thankful he turns around and leaves. Roman follows him out and shuts the door. The moment the lock engages, I sense Duke coming at my back.

I drop low and swipe my leg out to take him out at the ankles, feeling satisfaction when I make contact. "You're going to have to be quicker than that, you asshole."

He curses as he falls to the floor. I see the vein in his neck pulse just under the anchor tattoo. The moment he begins to stand, I kick him in the jaw, sending him back to the ground. "You made me like this."

"The thirst for blood was bred into you, little girl," he chuckles, staggering to his feet. Duke is six inches taller than me, but I've taken down bigger. He doesn't scare me anymore. "Your father was the same."

"I am nothing like my father," I snarl, tasting the lie on my tongue. "*You* did this to me."

"You were mine," he says, his eyes burning with anger. "I paid a pretty penny to your father for you to be my old lady, and you went and killed him.

If I hadn't stumbled on Vyper in Baton Rouge and put the pieces together, I wouldn't have found you."

"How did you know it was me?" I ask.

"Apparently, you have a reputation around here, and people in the underground know what you look like," he says. "Vyper obtained a photo of you from Jackson's club. That was the conformation I needed. He wanted to kill Jackson, and I wanted you returned to me."

"That will never happen," I growl. "Who was working for Vyper? How did they get a picture of me?" This could be an issue. I never thought they'd have someone working on the inside.

"Some waitress," he shrugs. "She likes cocaine, and we paid her really well."

"Was she the one in the car? The one who shot at Jackson's SUV?" I will find this woman and take her out myself. I don't know if Jackson can hear what's going on in this room, but he needs to know he has a traitor in his club.

"Marcy played her part well." He smiles as he walks toward me. "Do you really think you're going to kill me?"

"Yes," I answer.

I circle him and make sure my body is between him and the door. Duke may be talking now, but I don't trust him to take his punishment willingly. He eyes the door over my shoulder and stands tall. "You belong to me, Emily. It's inevitable. I will take you out of this building and we will return to Oregon."

"You have lost your fucking mind," I growl.

Before I can say another word, he reaches for me and grabs my wrist. I twist my arm out of his hold and reach for the knife I have tucked under my bra. He swipes his hand out, and the knife in my hand clatters to the ground and we freeze. He lunges for it at the same time I do.

I pounce on his arm and feel the stitches in my abdomen tear, but I grab the knife and start to stand. Duke kicks out at my ankles, but I'm quicker and take two short steps back. He jumps to his feet and lunges for me again.

"You bitch," he snarls when I palm the knife and slice him across the arm, drawing blood.

"Ah, too fast for you?" I taunt. I want him to engage me. I want to satisfy my own darkness while closing this chapter of my life.

"I'm going to enjoy having you as my old lady," he says, and lunges for me again. I slice him across the other arm this time, but it's deeper and blood starts running down the front of his arm as soon as I back away.

"Never," I reply, holding my fists up close to my face. The knife is in my palm and I tighten my hold on the blade. He surprises me when he spins around and lunges for me. I yelp when he takes me to the ground, and my side burns from the impact.

"Ah, ah, ah, Emily," he laughs as I roll my head to the side. He's holding my knife and his face looks victorious as he stands. "Time to come home."

I refuse to leave this place with him, and I stand to meet him face to face. Even if he gets me out of this building, Jackson's men are all over the place and will take him out.

"Jackson and his men will kill you before you even step foot off the property," I warn.

"Not if I have you as a hostage," he says, flipping the knife into the air and catching it the correct way. There's a gleam in his eye that tells me he believes he will get away.

"I will never go with you again." I see the moment he makes the decision to get his arms around me. I know he wants to get me in a choke hold and hold the knife to my throat so he can escape. I've been in many brawls with dangerous men, and I can tell when they are desperate to get away. They will take risky chances and hope for the best. His mind is scrambling because he knows without me, he will never be able to get out.

"I'm going to fuck your smart mouth until you do as I say," he says a second before he grabs ahold of my hair.

"Never!" I scream and reach around to my back where I have the gun tucked inside the back of my bra. I roll away from him and when he makes another move toward me, I pull the trigger and watch as a spot of red forms on his forehead and his gray matter splatters the wall behind him. Duke's body drops to the floor knees first. A second later, he goes limp and lands face first next to me on the concrete.

My body collapses from sheer exhaustion as the door to the room opens. Jackson, Roman, and Cyrus rush in and pause at the threshold. I take several deep breaths and roll to my knees, thankful they don't rush to my side. It takes me several seconds before I stand up with my back straight. I hand my gun to Roman as I pass and walk out into the darkness feeling like a weight of a thousand lifetimes has been lifted from my shoulders.

It's finally over.

"You're bleeding," Roman points out.

I look down at my stomach and see a few spots of red soaking through my shirt. It's not that bad. These men tend to be a little overbearingly protective when a woman is hurt. It's endearing, but I don't need their concern.

"Marcy," I snarl. "She was working with him."

"I heard." Jackson nods as he takes me into his arms, careful of my abdomen. "Moose went to go get her, but she took her own life."

"It's over," I breathe, looking over my shoulder at Duke's limp body on the ground. "Fuck."

"Yes, baby," Jackson replies. "It's over."

Epilogue
One Year Later
Morgan

Rain beats down on the roof of the heavily tinted SUV as we sit across the street from Tulane University. It's the last day of the week and students are rushing from one building to the next. All of them are armed with umbrellas to keep the rain off of their clothes.

"Are you ever going to approach her?" Jackson takes my hand into his and the strength and love he has for me is felt through our connection.

"No." I shake my head sadly. "Brooke is fine now. She's moved on."

"Why are we here?" he asks. The inquiry isn't one of frustration. Jackson is concerned for my well-being and has been since the day I walked into his club a year ago.

"I just want to make sure she's okay," I admit, sitting up a little straighter when she comes into view.

Brook Hasselbeck looks like any other college student, but unlike the others, a man walks with her. They don't hold hands, but I can see the small lift to the corner of her mouth when he speaks. She looks at him with trust and love.

The man is her bodyguard. I don't even need to be told about him, because I can read them like a book. This man is armed with a concealed piece, but he's carrying a book bag as if he is a student, too. He will stop at nothing to keep her safe.

I smile when they stop under a tree just outside the building. Brooke brushes her dark-blonde hair over her shoulder, and the man lifts his hand to her cheek, using his thumb to stroke her jaw. He leans down and kisses her softly on the lips before stepping back. They both enter the building and are gone from sight.

"She really is doing okay," I observe. She found her happy ending.

"Yes, she is," Jackson replies.

"She looks happy." I smile and turn toward Jackson when he touches my hand. He has this look on his face like he is worried about something.

"What?"

"Are *you* happy?"

"I've never been happier in my life," I say with a hint of confusion. "Why are you asking me this?"

"Are you ever going to stop hunting them?" he asks. It'd been an argument with us for a while now. He loves me and knows I can protect myself. Unfortunately, his need to protect me sometimes overrides his trust in my ability to do what I do.

"No, Jackson." I sigh and twist in my seat so I can look at him dead on. "Unfortunately, for everyone I take off the streets, another takes his place."

"I know," he whispers and presses his lips to mine. "I love you, my little huntress, and I support you in whatever you do."

"Thank you, Jax," I smirk, knowing I am the only one who can get away with calling him by that dreaded nickname.

When my phone rings, I don't even let out a harsh breath when I see it's an unknown caller. I believe I've become numb to the violence that plagues this city. Assault is a daily occurrence, and it has to be stopped.

I've made it my life's goal to protect these women until I am no longer able to do so. After that, I don't know who will take my place.

"Hello?" I answer.

"Um…hello?" the shaky female voice says over the line. From the background sounds, I can tell she's in the Quarter.

"Yes?" I answer as a way of a test. I don't ever tell my name over the phone or start the conversation.

"My friend has been hurt really bad," she sniffles. "Can you help me find the man who hurt her?"

"Give me the information," I answer, reaching into the front seat of the SUV for a pen and piece of paper. Keon keeps a stash for me for just this thing. "I'll help you."

"Her name is Ashlynn," the caller hiccups when the tears can no longer be held at bay, "and her boyfriend beat her up really bad."

"Where is she now?" I ask.

"At the hospital," she answers. "I don't care what you do, or how much money it will cost me, but I want him taken out. My friend is scared for her life."

"I won't let him hurt your friend ever again," I promise.

It's a promise I've made to over two hundred

women since I arrived in New Orleans, and it's one that I live by to make sure the women in this city are protected.

The End...

Other Books by Theresa Hissong:

About Theresa Hissong:

Theresa is a mother of two and the wife of a retired Air Force Master Sergeant. After seventeen years traveling the country, moving from base to base, the family has settled their roots back in Theresa's home town of Olive Branch, MS, where she enjoys her time going to concerts and camping with her family.

After almost three years of managing a retail bookstore, Theresa has gone behind the scenes to write romantic stories with flare. She enjoys spending her afternoons daydreaming of the perfect love affair and takes those ideas to paper.

Look for other exciting reads…coming very soon!